W9-CNB-069

Praise for L. A. Witt's
The Distance Between Us

"The Distance Between Us packs an emotional wallop that is perfectly balanced with blazing hot sex. Ethan, Rhett, and Kieran will linger in your hearts and thoughts long after the last page is turned."

~ *Whipped Cream Erotic Romance Reviews*

"If you're looking for a book that's different, a lot of fun, mucho recreational sex between three hot men who can't get enough, then you should pick up this book."

~ *Reviews by Jessewave*

Look for these titles by
L. A. Witt

Now Available:

Nine-tenths of the Law
A.J.'s Angel

The Distance Between Us

L. A. Witt

SAMHAIN
PUBLISHING

Samhain Publishing, Ltd.
577 Mulberry Street, Suite 1520
Macon, GA 31201
www.samhainpublishing.com

The Distance Between Us
Copyright © 2011 by L. A. Witt
Print ISBN: 978-1-60928-125-0
Digital ISBN: 978-1-60928-136-6

Editing by Linda Ingmanson
Cover by Scott Carpenter

This book is a work of fiction. The names, characters, places, and incidents are products of the writer's imagination or have been used fictitiously and are not to be construed as real. Any resemblance to persons, living or dead, actual events, locale or organizations is entirely coincidental.

All Rights Are Reserved. No part of this book may be used or reproduced in any manner whatsoever without written permission, except in the case of brief quotations embodied in critical articles and reviews.

First Samhain Publishing, Ltd. electronic publication: July 2010
First Samhain Publishing, Ltd. print publication: June 2011

Dedication

To my brutally honest, quitcher-wangsting, *gerronwi'*
gerrinit writ writing partner, Nichola, and my equally brutal,
pull-no-punches, beta reader, Libbie. My writing would be
nothing without you awesomely talented ladies.

— L.

Chapter One

When I opened the front door one Saturday afternoon, I expected to meet Kieran Frost, an applicant for the room for rent in the house I shared with my ex-boyfriend.

What I *didn't* expect was to meet Kieran Frost, owner of the most stunning green eyes I'd ever seen. He was gorgeous. Simply fucking gorgeous. The tight jeans and black leather jacket didn't help any, drawing my attention to his broad shoulders and narrow hips. I hadn't necessarily assumed that our potential roommate would be unattractive, but I certainly hadn't bargained for this.

Thankfully, he broke the silence before I had a chance to make a complete idiot of myself.

"I'm Kieran," he said, extending a hand. "I'm here to look at the room for rent. I assume this is the right place?"

"Yes, this is the place." I shook his hand. "Rhett Solomon."

He grinned. "I suppose I shouldn't make any jokes about *Gone with the Wind*."

"You wouldn't be the first, you won't be the last." I laughed. "Especially once you hear my sister's name."

"Your sister's name is Scarlett?" His eyes widened.

I chuckled. "Guess what my mom's favorite book was."

"You're kidding."

"Nope. Anyway, come in, come in." I gestured inside. As he walked past me, I couldn't help but cast a surreptitious glance at him. A mistake, of course, because he was just as sexy from the back as the front. *Lead me not into temptation...*

He didn't seem to notice my staring, though, because he was more enthralled with the house.

"Wow," he said. "This is a nice place."

"Yeah, we like to think so." I shut the door behind us and gestured for him to follow me down the hall. "Here, let me show you the room that's available." I led him down the hall, silently wondering if this was a good idea. We needed a tenant, but I was frustrated enough—for very different reasons—with Ethan still living here. I wasn't sure I could handle being around Kieran *and* Ethan.

Desperate times, desperate measures.

I opened the door to the third bedroom and turned to say something to him, but he quickly glanced away and cleared his throat as if I'd caught him looking at something he shouldn't have been. Like me. I couldn't be sure, but even in the dim light of the hallway, I swore his cheeks darkened a little.

Wishful thinking, Solomon. I gestured toward the bedroom. "This is it."

He didn't look at me on his way into the room, but the sunlight coming in through the window confirmed my suspicion. There was a little extra pink in his cheeks and *good God, Kieran, you must have sold your soul for cheekbones like that.*

He checked out the room, and I answered questions when he had them. All the while, I tried to convince myself there was no point in looking. Nor was there any point in entertaining any kind of fantasy about what went on in his mind when he'd looked at me. We were to be roommates. He was an extra check every month to help us pay down the mortgage until Ethan and I could sell the damned place and go our separate ways.

I pressed my tongue stud against the roof of my mouth as I often did when I was nervous. This was ridiculous. From what Ethan said after speaking to him on the phone, Kieran was twenty-five. A full fourteen years my junior. Hell, he was closer to my daughter's age than mine. He was too young, I was too newly single. *Oh, but what I wouldn't give for a night with someone that hot.*

"I like it," he said, nodding and giving the room one last look.

"I should show you the rest of the house, then." I smiled, hoping I hid all the thoughts running through my mind. We stepped out into the hallway.

"The bathroom's the next door down on the left." I pointed in its direction. "Between—" I hesitated. "Between our bedrooms. We'll be sharing that bathroom."

He nodded, but said nothing. I quickly changed the subject before I spent too much time thinking about Kieran in the same shower I'd be using.

"You're welcome to any room in the house besides our bedrooms. *Mi casa, su casa.* All we ask is that you replace anything you use in the kitchen, and we'll do the same."

"Fair enough."

"We don't care about having people over," I said. "Obviously, the usual requests about keeping things clean and not making too much noise, but otherwise, we're pretty easygoing about everything."

"I work nights anyway," he said. "I won't wake anyone up when I get in at two or three in the morning, will I?"

I shook my head. "Ethan sleeps like the dead, and I keep

fairly late hours. Anyway, let me show you the rest of the place. Downstairs, it's mostly the garage and a storage room, plus an office that we don't use much anymore." I gestured up the stairs. "Ethan's bedroom and the other bathroom are up there. There's also a home gym."

"Oh?" His eyes lit up. "Can I see the gym?"

"Sure." On the way up the stairs, I added, "Not exactly sure what possessed us to drag all of this shit upstairs. I had half a mind to put the living room up there and leave all the equipment downstairs."

"Probably got a workout hauling it all upstairs," he said, chuckling.

I glanced over my shoulder. "You have *no* idea." I pushed open the door to the rec room that had been converted into a gym.

"Oh, wow." He wandered amidst the weight racks, treadmills and multi-purpose machines. "Damn, this alone is worth the rent." He looked at me. "Guess I won't bother with a gym membership, then."

"Yeah, it all paid for itself pretty quickly. You're welcome to use any of it."

"Sweet." He looked over the rack of plates. "I've been meaning to get into some weight training." His eyes flicked up. "I don't suppose I could talk either of you into showing me a thing or two, could I?"

Oh God. I coughed, then shrugged, trying to look casual. "Sure, yeah. We both know our way around the weight room, so..." Another shrug, pretending I wasn't simultaneously thanking God for the opportunity and pleading for the strength to resist such sweet, sweet temptation.

And the more I pictured Kieran, sweating and panting in my home gym, the more I—

"Why don't I show you the kitchen and living room?" I said. "Then we can go over all the paperwork."

Downstairs, on the way across the sprawling living room, he stopped in his tracks. "Wow, that's quite a view."

I paused and turned. He was looking out the sliding glass door, so I gestured toward it. "Go out and have a look."

We went out onto the balcony, and he leaned against the railing, taking in the panoramic view of Lake Union and Queen Anne Hill.

"So how long does it take for the novelty of seeing the Space Needle every day to wear off?"

I laughed. "You're not a Seattle native, are you?"

He shook his head. "Just moved up here from Sacramento."

"Trust me, you won't even notice the damned thing after a week or two."

"I take it you're a native?" he asked as we walked back into the house.

"Moved here a few years ago. From Portland."

"So you're a Northwesterner. Washington, Oregon, it's all the same."

I looked over my shoulder and raised an eyebrow. "And Sacramento and LA are the same too, right?"

"Hey, those are fightin' words." He laughed. We stepped into the kitchen, and he whistled. "I think this kitchen is bigger than my last apartment."

I folded my arms and leaned against the counter. "Was one of the major selling points of the house."

"I can imagine. How long have you had it, anyway?"

"Just over a year." Some bitterness crept into my tone, but I tried to push it back. I looked around the kitchen and living room. "I hate to sell it, but—"

"You're selling it?" He ran his fingers along the beveled edge of the black granite countertop. "Man, they'd have to pry a place like this out of my cold dead hands."

"Well, it's not going up right away. Depending on what the market does, probably in a year or two." Inwardly, I cringed, digging my tongue stud into the roof of my mouth and trying not to groan. Another year or two of living with Ethan. No matter how many times we'd discussed this, no matter how much I convinced myself there was little choice, the very thought of sharing a house for even another month was enough to nauseate me.

I shifted my weight. "Anyway, we won't be selling any time soon, so don't worry about us throwing you out." *Though if you lick your lips like that again, you might have to worry about me throwing you down on—*

The front door opened. Kieran's head turned, and my jaw tightened.

"That would be Ethan," I said through my teeth. Kieran shot me a puzzled glance, but, before he could say anything, Ethan appeared in the doorway to the kitchen.

I watched Kieran's face as he drank in the sight of Ethan, and I couldn't blame him for the catch of his breath. There were plenty of things I could have said about Ethan, but I definitely couldn't say he was bad looking. Those devilish brown eyes were what had attracted me to him in the first place and, even after everything we'd been through, they still made my pulse jump. Though he was forty-one, his dark hair had just a hint of silver at his temples. The time he spent in the gym was evident in the powerful build of his shoulders and the perfectly flat stomach. I hadn't seen him without a shirt on in a long, long time, but he'd had a six-pack for years, and most likely still did.

Even with the button-down shirt and blazer he wore now, he was obviously fit.

Pity I could barely stand the sight of him, because he certainly wasn't hard on the eyes.

"You must be Kieran." He extended a hand. "Ethan Mallory. I hope he hasn't told you too much about me." His eyes darted toward me and one side of his mouth lifted in his trademark smirk. That look used to make my knees weak. Now it irritated me. Or maybe that was just Ethan's presence. Either way, he was here and I wished he wasn't.

Kieran shook Ethan's hand. "He's just finished showing me around the house. I still can't believe you guys are going to sell this place."

Ethan dropped his gaze and shrugged. "Well, you know how things happen. Sometimes it's just time to move on."

Kieran's eyes shifted back and forth between us, something like alarm in his expression.

I quickly changed the subject. "So, you're working at Wilde's?"

He nodded. "They just hired me on as a bartender."

Ethan's smirk returned. "Hey, that means we can brag to our friends that we've got a Wilde's bartender living with us."

Kieran laughed. "I could think of more prestigious bragging rights."

"Hardly." I chuckled. "Wilde's is the Coyote Ugly of gay bars in Seattle. If you can get a job behind that bar—"

"Let's just say it's not quite the same as working at one of the other local dives," Ethan cut in. "They only hire the best." I wondered if Kieran caught the quick down-up sweep of Ethan's eyes. The look was anything but subtle, but if Kieran noticed, he didn't react. *Jesus, Ethan, let the guy sign the lease before you start hitting on him, would you?*

"Well, I'd definitely like to rent the room," Kieran said. "Where do I sign?"

I picked up the paperwork off the counter. "Everything's here. Just need first and last month's rent, and have you sign or initial everywhere that's highlighted." I handed him the papers and a pen.

Ethan and I left the kitchen so Kieran could take care of paperwork without us looking over his shoulder. As we stepped out onto the balcony, the cool air from inside followed us. It was warm outside, even for late spring, but the space between us was cold. We both looked out at the city. I'd long since stopped noticing the Space Needle, but it suddenly fascinated me, if only as something to look at that wasn't Ethan.

"I'm checking into some new jobs," he said suddenly. After a moment, he added, "Back in Toronto."

I lost interest in the Space Needle and turned to him. "Toronto? But what about this? With the house?"

He shrugged. "I'll keep paying my share of it. I assume you won't object to me being out of the house as long as the money's still coming in."

Oh, you aren't wrong there. "It's your call. If you do move, we should put it on the market sooner than later."

"If that was a realistic option, it would be on the market right now," he muttered. "And we wouldn't be in this situation." He paused. "Look, it'll cost me more money in the long run, but I'd like to be a bit closer to my family. I don't exactly have a reason to stay here." The bitterness in his voice set my teeth on edge.

"I guess it's a good thing I wasn't planning to move back to Portland any time soon," I growled.

He rolled his eyes. "If you were, you haven't said a word about it to me. I'm not planning my life around yours anymore."

"No, we're both planning our lives around this fucking house. You just found a way out before I did."

"Look, the sooner we go our separate ways, the better," he said. "We'll be out of each other's hair. Once we get rid of the house, then we can truly be done with it, but that's out of our hands right now." As much as I didn't like being saddled with the house after he left, at least he'd still be paying for it, and he was right. We'd be out of each other's hair.

"Well, just let me know what happens then."

"It's not set in stone," he said. "I'm sending my résumé to a few places, but I haven't even gotten any calls. It'll be at least a couple of months. But I wanted to let you know."

"Much appreciated," I said dryly.

He glanced over his shoulder and the smirk—along with my annoyance—came back. "I have to say, I think I'll enjoy this view for the next few months, though."

My annoyance turned into something else, tightening in my chest and throat as I tapped my tongue stud against my teeth. Was that—no, it couldn't be. I'd only just met Kieran and I was eagerly awaiting the day Ethan moved out. Why the hell was I *jealous*?

The sliding glass door opened, and we both turned.

"I think this is everything." Kieran handed me the paperwork. "Is a check okay for the deposit?"

"Check is fine." I flipped through the pages to make sure everything was signed and initialed as it needed to be. "Yeah, looks like we're all set."

"So when's he moving in?" Ethan asked.

"Lease technically starts on the first." I looked at Kieran.

"But when works best for you?"

"My nights off next week are Wednesday and Thursday," he said. "It would be a day or two early, but—"

"Works for me," Ethan said. His smirk turned into a grin. "The sooner the better."

Kieran smiled at him. "Why don't we make it Thursday, then?"

"Sounds good," Ethan said. "I'll take the day off and help you move in." To me, he said, "I assume you're okay with this?" From his tone, I didn't imagine he cared about my opinion either way.

Day one, and you'll already be alone in the house with him. Nice. I forced a smile. "Thursday sounds fine." I reached out to shake Kieran's hand again. "Welcome to our house."

Chapter Two

On Thursday night, I had to work late. By the time I got home, Kieran had finished moving into his room and was relaxing in the living room with Ethan and a bottle of wine.

Ethan sat with one knee up on the cushion, allowing him to turn and face Kieran completely. His arm was across the back of the couch, close to Kieran, but not touching him. Not touching him *yet*. If I knew the look in his eyes as well as I thought I did, he was one flirtatious ice-breaking comment away from a hand on Kieran's knee.

Kieran looked over his shoulder and smiled at me. "Hey, Rhett."

"Hey," I said.

Ethan gave a polite nod, but impatience was written all over the set of his jaw and the way he tapped his loose fist against the back of the couch. I lifted my eyebrow and tightened my lips just enough to let him know it hadn't escaped my notice without tipping off Kieran.

We made quick, polite small talk, then I left them to their conversation and went into my bedroom. I could have stayed and toyed with Ethan, casually interfering with his pursuit of our new roommate, but as amusing as his frustration might be, being in his presence wasn't worth this tension.

I changed clothes, grabbed my MP3 player and went

upstairs to work out. Cranking up the music so I wouldn't accidentally catch a stray laugh from downstairs, I got on the treadmill and tried to concentrate on my run. Of course, running was a somewhat mindless activity. Usually, that was my favorite thing about running. It gave me the chance to zone out and let my thoughts wander, relaxing my mind while my body worked.

Tonight, I wished running required a hell of a lot more concentration. Maybe then my mind wouldn't keep wandering back downstairs.

After I finished my run, I started on the weights. At least that wasn't such a passive activity and required more concentration than running, but even that couldn't get my mind off Ethan and Kieran. More than once, I had to remind myself to slow down, to focus on form and technique rather than just taking my irritation out on my lifts. The last thing I needed was a pulled muscle on top of this teeth-grinding frustration.

Kieran had barely moved into the house, and already Ethan was moving in for the kill. I had no way of knowing if he was just *that* attracted to Kieran—and for that I certainly couldn't blame him—or if he was seizing the opportunity before I could make a move.

Or maybe he was just horny. It had only been a few weeks since we'd split, but we hadn't had sex in months.

Whatever the case, I couldn't blame him for going after Kieran. I couldn't blame him, but I could certainly be irritated with him. I wanted to wring his neck, but really, I couldn't justify my anger toward him. We were both single now. Every man for himself.

This ought to make our living arrangement a little less bearable. Not only was I living with the man who dumped me, I got to live with him while he fucked the first guy I'd set my sights on in a damned decade.

I sighed as I put a pair of dumbbells back on the rack. I was getting way ahead of myself. My mind already had Ethan and Kieran tearing off clothes and breaking furniture, but as far as I knew, reality still had them on the couch. Fully dressed and flirting. No, talking. They were just *talking*.

Then again, Ethan would probably change that in fairly short order. The man moved fast when he saw something he wanted.

All he has to do is kiss him and it's all over, I thought as I put plates on a bar for a dead lift. Ethan had a kiss that was second to none. Once Kieran got a taste of it, he was Ethan's to lose.

After my workout, I showered and went downstairs for a drink. Ethan and Kieran were no longer in the living room, having moved out to the balcony.

They both rested their forearms on the railing and exchanged lingering glances as they talked. I couldn't hear what they were saying, but the lack of distance between them spoke volumes.

I shook my head and went into the kitchen.

Moments later, the sliding glass door to the balcony opened and closed. Ethan strolled into the kitchen looking pretty damned pleased with himself and set an empty wine bottle on the island.

"Have you had a chance to chat with Kieran?" His smug grin told me he already knew the answer. *He's lived here for a matter of hours, all of which have been in your company, douchebag.*

"Aside from showing him around the house, no, can't say I have. Haven't had the opportunity."

"You really should." The grin broadened. "You know, when you have the opportunity."

"Duly noted," I muttered into my water bottle.

"He's quite a guy." Ethan furrowed his brow as he looked through the wine rack. "And I can definitely see why Wilde's took him on. Jesus, you should see the man without his shirt."

I choked on my drink. "What? You mean you—"

"While we were moving stuff into the house." He clicked his tongue and rolled his eyes. "Christ, Rhett, do you think I'd move in that quickly?" He pulled a wine bottle off the rack and smirked as he reached for the corkscrew. "I do have a little more finesse than that, don't you think?"

"Mm-hmm." I bit back the snide comments that wanted so badly to come out.

He smirked, and there was no doubt in my mind he was toying with me. Taunting me. As if brazenly flirting with our hot new roommate right under my nose wasn't enough.

"Well, anyway." He picked up the open wine bottle and started toward the doorway. "Have a good night."

"Will do." I raised my water bottle in a mock toast. "Same to you."

He winked at me, and I clenched my teeth.

As the sliding glass door opened and closed again, I shook my head before taking another drink. There was no sense getting annoyed about all of this. Kieran was hot. Any red-blooded gay male would go after him in a heartbeat, so why should Ethan hold back on my account?

And really, Kieran was attractive, but chances were I was just attracted to anything that wasn't Ethan right now. I didn't relish the idea of being back out on the dating scene for the first time in ten years. I wasn't even sure where to start. A hot, single man living in my house seemed like as good a place as any.

I could always find a woman, I thought on my way out of the kitchen. After all, I hadn't been with a woman in ages. Glancing at Ethan, I muttered to myself, "Then again, I haven't been with a *man* in a good long time either."

I closed my bedroom door and sat on the bed with my laptop. I was half-tempted to scour some of the online dating sites, if only to find someone worth a one- or two-night stand, but the very thought made me groan. As much as I wanted to get laid, it probably wasn't such a good idea just yet. Ethan evidently had no problem jumping right back into the game, but I wasn't so sure if I was quite ready for it.

Instead, I checked e-mail and instant messaged my daughter for a while. She was in the last quarter of her freshman year in college, and listening to her talk about midterms, classes and dorm drama was a welcome distraction from Kieran and Ethan. I missed having her here in the house— though her dorm was only about twenty minutes away—but it was probably just as well she wasn't living here now.

Eventually, my eyes were too tired to focus on the screen, so I said good night to my daughter, closed my laptop and went to bed.

And just like running, sleep turned out to be the perfect venue to think about the last two people I wanted to think about.

Chapter Three

I was somewhere in that hazy state between asleep and awake when something brought me back to full awareness. Blinking in the dark, I tried to locate the sound that had pulled me into consciousness.

Down the hall, the sliding glass door hissed, then clicked shut. Shuffling footsteps moved across the hardwood floor of the living room, toward the hallway. No voices, just footsteps. Uneven, almost stumbling. Bumping into furniture, struggling for balance. I wondered just how many bottles of wine Ethan had gone through. He wasn't usually the type to get fall down drunk, particularly not while he was trying to lay the charm on someone. Or maybe it was Kieran. He wasn't as familiar with the layout of the house, and since there was no strip of light under my door, he was probably trying to work his way through the darkness.

Fabric brushed against plaster. Again, with a little more force this time. Definitely Kieran. Between the dark and the wine, he must—

A low murmur, something I couldn't understand, ending in enough of a lilt to indicate a question.

Then a response. The reply was deeper, quieter, so low I almost felt it rather than heard it. And it was a voice I knew all too well: The hoarse growl of a very aroused Ethan.

Fabric rustled again and they continued down the hall, past Kieran's bedroom, toward the stairs.

You two didn't waste any time, did you?

For the first time, I was aware of every creak of the stairs and wished we'd put down carpet. At least then I wouldn't hear their shoes tapping and shuffling, occasionally even squeaking, as they worked their way up to the third floor.

The house was absolutely silent except for the nearly—but not completely—inaudible sounds they made on their way into Ethan's bedroom.

Ethan's bedroom, which was directly over mine.

I closed my eyes and let out a frustrated breath. One of the selling points of this house was that it was in an exceptionally quiet part of Capitol Hill. Just this once, I wished we'd bought a place right beside the freeway. At least then the roar of traffic would have been enough to drown out the muffled sounds of my ex getting it on with our new roommate.

My eyes tracked across the ceiling, following the sound of their footsteps as if I could see them. Pulling off clothes, stumbling over each other's feet, kissing like only Ethan knew how to kiss.

I shivered. It didn't matter how or why we'd split or how we felt about each other, the fact remained that no one kissed like Ethan Mallory. *Oh, Kieran, you lucky son of a bitch.*

The lips were only the beginning. Right about now, Kieran was probably discovering just how many erogenous zones Ethan could find on someone's neck, or what his perpetually stubbled jaw felt like when skin brushed skin, or what Ethan's voice felt like when he moaned into a deep kiss. I ran my tongue stud along my teeth, remembering the way Ethan would tease it with the tip of his tongue.

Just wait until you find out what else his mouth can do, lad.

23

They stopped moving. I could hear nothing except for the beating of my own heart, but my mind's eye filled in everything that was probably going on. If I knew Ethan, he was anything but silent right then, kissing his way up and down Kieran's neck while whispering in great detail all the ways he'd make him beg for more.

And if I knew Ethan, he wasn't exaggerating. Whatever he said he would do, he did. Promises of a rough, hard fuck, or a long, spine-melting blowjob, even a gentle, oiled massage that would no doubt lead to much more. I could almost feel Ethan's lips and voice against my neck as he breathed all his promises.

The distant, muffled sound of a belt buckle made me shiver. Clothes hit the floor; jeans, I guessed, if I could hear it that clearly. Footsteps moved above me, then bedsprings creaked softly.

I closed my eyes again. I wanted to be angry, I wanted to be jealous, but just the thought of either of those men, naked and horny, made me want to be *there*. And whether I liked it or not, my body wanted to be there too.

Reaching under the covers, I closed my hand around my cock and stroked slowly, barely even breathing so as not to drown out the faint sounds from upstairs.

They were mostly silent now, save for the occasional gentle creak of the bed accommodating movement. Knowing Ethan, he probably had his hand and mouth around Kieran's cock. He'd be stroking and sucking, his occasional enthusiastic, aroused moan sending Kieran into the stratosphere. The man gave head like he could feel everything he did on his own cock.

Biting my lip, I stroked my cock the way I remembered Ethan doing it: Slower, faster, slower, faster, pausing now and again just to keep me on the edge. I tried to imagine Kieran's face, his eyes screwed shut and his lips parted with breathless, soundless cries, until he reached that point of no return and his eyes—those incredible, hypnotic green eyes—flew open just as he came in Ethan's mouth.

I could barely breathe, taking uneven gasps whenever I could think to do so. Above me, more motion, more urgency and speed. Kieran was probably right there, getting close just as I was. What I wouldn't have given to have been the one about to make him come like that.

Closing my eyes, I held my breath as the faint, distant vibration of Kieran's voice slowly crescendoed into a moan, then a deeper sound and, just before I couldn't hold back anymore, I realized it wasn't Kieran's voice at all. Ethan came with a whimper that I could barely hear, but it was enough, and in that same instant, I came too.

When I could finally draw a breath, my body relaxed and my spine sank back down to the bed. I hadn't even realized I'd arched my back like that, but the force of my orgasm had nearly levitated my entire body. With a trembling hand, I reached for the tissues on my bedside table.

Above me, there were more sounds of movement. Then, the all-too-familiar sound of the nightstand drawer opening, then closing. I couldn't help but shudder, imagining Kieran fucking Ethan. Not only that, but by the time Kieran was done, Ethan would probably have recovered. He may have been a few months away from forty-two, but he had the kind of stamina that rivaled men half his age.

If Kieran could keep up with him like I could, the sun would be coming up around the time they finally collapsed.

Ethan's bedframe groaned in protest of more movement, then fell into a rhythmic creak, filling my mind with all manner of sexy, frustrating images.

If Kieran could keep up with him like I could, they were going to kill me before this night was over.

Chapter Four

I was halfway through my first cup of coffee when Ethan came downstairs. I wondered if he'd gloat, if he'd quietly flaunt his conquest, or if it would be business as usual. Would he flash me a smug grin or pretend that nothing out of the ordinary had happened above my bedroom last night?

As soon as he walked into the kitchen, I had my answer. He didn't say a word, didn't even look at me, but he had on a pair of jeans and nothing else.

Ethan never wandered around without a shirt. *Never.* Except, apparently, when he was sporting a few battle scars from a rough, wild roll in the hay. They were faint, the hints of red and purple on his sides and shoulders, but they were there.

"Morning," he said. His face was a little pale, especially compared to the circles under his eyes, but he was all smiles. "Sleep well?"

"Always do," I muttered into my coffee cup. *Oh, sweet irony. You're the one with dark circles under your eyes, and I'm the one who feels like I haven't slept in a month.*

"Glad to hear it." His smugness set my teeth on edge. He may or may not have known that I knew about his night with Kieran, but he was definitely gloating about it.

Ethan turned to pour himself a cup of coffee, and I nearly choked on mine. Two more bruises, almost mirror images of each other, peeked out from his jeans. Darker than the other marks, they were a few inches apart on either side of his spine just above the small of his back, and I'd have bet money that if I laid my hands over them, my thumbs would fit perfectly on top of the marks while my fingers grabbed onto his hips.

He turned around and I looked into my coffee cup, pretending I hadn't been staring. When he again turned away to get something out of the refrigerator, I stole another glance.

I could have been mistaken, but the red, crescent-shaped mark just above his collarbone looked an awful lot like a bite. *So Mr. Frost likes it rough, does he?* I shivered. *You lucky bastards. Both of you.*

We made some small talk, which wasn't terse and cold like it usually was. At least that was a silver lining; if getting laid made Ethan more pleasant to be around, then at least I was getting some benefit out of it.

After a while, he drained his coffee, set his cup in the sink and headed out of the kitchen, pausing in the doorway to twist a crick out of his back.

I couldn't help but chuckle. *Age catching up with you, Ethan?*

A few minutes later, Kieran came into the kitchen. Thankfully, he'd opted to wear jeans and a shirt. Ethan was bad enough; I wasn't sure I could handle a half-naked Kieran.

As it was, being in the same room with him was more than sufficient to make my lungs forget how to work. He looked just like he had the day before, but now I knew what he sounded like when he came. I knew what kinds of sounds he'd gotten out of Ethan. He sported dark circles under his eyes, too, a reminder of how long he'd gone on and on and on last night. He probably even had a mark or two on his back, hips and shoulders, so I was again thankful he'd worn a shirt.

"Morning." I sipped my coffee, then set it on the counter.

"Morning," he said as he poured himself some.

"You working tonight?" I asked just to make conversation.

He nodded. "Yeah, I don't have another night off until Tuesday." His voice had a vague hoarseness about it, and I didn't have to ask why.

"How do you like it there?" I asked. "At Wilde's?"

"Loving it. I'm loving Seattle so far too. Not as cold and rainy as everyone said it would be."

I chuckled. "It's spring. Just wait until fall."

"That bad, huh?"

"It's not too bad." I shrugged. "Just be ready for a few more grey days than you're used to."

"Lovely." He rolled his eyes and sipped his coffee. Then he looked at me with a sly grin. "Weather aside, if I'd known there were so many good-looking men in this city, I'd have moved here a long time ago." His eyes made a quick down-up sweep before meeting mine again.

My cheeks burning, I laughed softly. "Well, this place has its perks."

"I'm not going to argue with that," he said into his coffee cup. He set the cup down and ran the tip of his tongue along the inside of his lower lip. "I think I'm going to like living here."

"In Seattle?" I raised an eyebrow. "Or here?"

The grin turned into a smirk that rivaled Ethan's. "Both."

I swallowed. *My, my, you don't let the grass grow from one conquest to the next, do you?*

"So how long have you and Ethan been roommates?" he asked.

Define "roommates" in this case, my friend. I pursed my

29

lips. "We've, um, we've lived together for a while. Quite a few years, actually."

"Really? I've never lived with anyone for very long. Two years, tops."

I shrugged. "I'm used to it, I guess. My daughter moved out last year, but otherwise, it's been just the two of us." My emphasis on "just the two of us" seemed to stop him in his tracks and I could almost hear the penny dropping in his mind.

"*Oh.*" He chewed his lip and, for a moment, I thought he was going to ask, but instead, he drained his coffee cup and set it in the sink. A full minute of uncomfortable silence ticked by. Then I opened my mouth to speak, intending to explain what Ethan and I were before and what we were now, but Kieran cleared his throat and said, "Well, I'd better run. I've got some errands before I go to work tonight."

I hesitated, then nodded. There would be time to explain everything later. After Kieran left the kitchen, I finished my coffee and got ready for work. All the while, I wondered why Ethan hadn't told Kieran about our past relationship.

Then I sighed, having answered my own question.

He hadn't told Kieran because even though we lived together, I was now a part of Ethan's past.

Chapter Five

That night, I stood out on the balcony, watching the sun go down behind the city. After yet another sniping match with Ethan about bills and bullshit, I needed some air. He'd long since gone out for the evening, but his presence seemed to linger in the house, and it was stifling.

Shortly after darkness fell, the sliding glass door opened. I was off to the side on the balcony where I wasn't visible from the living room, and when I turned around, Kieran jumped as he stepped outside.

"Oh," he said. "I didn't know you were out here."

"It's okay." I gestured toward the railing. "Plenty of room for two." My heart raced. Just living in the same house with him was murder on my blood pressure, but being within the confines of the tiny balcony was too much.

As he leaned against it, I glanced at him and my breath caught. No longer backlit by the light from the living room, he was visible as more than just a silhouette, and he was dressed for work. In true Wilde's bartender style, he looked absolutely stunning. The jacketless tuxedo, particularly with its slimming black cummerbund, made any man look sexy, but the men behind the bar at that club were hot anyway. Kieran was no exception.

"What?" he said.

Realizing I was staring, I shook my head and looked away. "Nothing."

"You sure?"

Even in the low light, I had no doubt the color of my face gave me away, so there was no point in denying it. Resting my forearms on the railing, I looked at him. "I just didn't realize you'd be dressed for work."

He looked down at his clothes, then gave me a puzzled look.

"Let's just say you wear it well."

"Thanks." He laughed softly.

No, no, thank you. We both fell silent, but that silence didn't last long.

"So, if it's not too personal of me to ask," he said suddenly, "I'm curious about you and Ethan."

I cocked my head. "What about us?" Then I remembered our conversation that morning.

He shifted his weight, looking out at the city. "I mean, the two of you, are you—" He cut himself off, swallowing hard. "Do you have a—"

"Relationship?"

Nodding, he finally managed a glance at me, eyebrows raised and cheeks darkening slightly. "Yeah."

Funny you should ask, now that you've already fucked him. I cleared my throat. "We had a relationship. Now we're just..." Stuck together? Trapped? Ready to kill each other? "...friends."

"Oh. To be honest, I've been trying to figure you guys out since I moved in. And after this morning. I didn't want to be intrusive, but..."

Crisis of conscience after going to bed with him? I shrugged. "It's a bit of a strange setup right now, so I can understand if it confused you."

"Just a little." He laughed quietly. "So how long were you together?"

I took a breath. "Ten years."

He whistled. "Wow. And I thought I'd just gotten out of a long relationship."

"Oh really? How long?"

"Three years. Called it quits a few months ago. That's why I moved up here. You know, needed a change of scenery."

I looked out at the city. *I hear Toronto's nice this time of year,* I wanted to mutter. Silently, I berated myself for my attitude. All three of us were single. He had every right to hook up with Ethan. I had no business being jealous. Even if Kieran *had* flirted with me and Ethan *had* quietly gloated about their little tryst, I had no right to be jealous. For that matter, we'd done nothing to establish to Kieran that we'd ever been in a relationship, so he had no reason to be concerned when he slept with Ethan. I was just jealous that Ethan got to him first, so there was no sense holding it against Kieran.

"Anyway, I guess I just wanted to make sure I wasn't, you know..." He bit his lip and stared out at the skyline.

"Getting involved with someone else's man?" I asked.

He turned so fast I thought his neck would snap. "What? You—" He gulped. "He told you?"

"No, he didn't say anything." I laughed. "I, um, figured it out."

"Oh." He was quiet for a moment. "So, it doesn't bother you? If he and I are, you know..."

"Fucking?"

His cheeks darkened even more. "Yeah. Fucking."

It does bother me, but only because I want you so bad it

33

hurts. "Nah," I said. "Really, he and I are done. I don't own him." *I don't want him. I want you.*

He nodded slowly and pursed his lips. "I was just curious."

"So if you don't mind my asking..." I wasn't sure I wanted to know, but what the hell? "What *is* going on between you two?"

"Nothing, really. I mean, I'm not looking to get involved with anyone anytime soon. You know, nothing serious. Just having a little fun right now."

"I don't blame you there." I looked across the lake again. "I think I'm going to stay single for a while, myself. Maybe play the field a bit. This relationship crap can go to hell."

"I hear that. Way too much headache."

I laughed. "No kidding."

"So, he and I are just, you know..." He cleared his throat. "Anyway, I just feel better knowing it doesn't bother you. I'd hate for things to get weird with all of us living together."

The very fact that we're all living together is weird enough. "Don't worry about it. Besides, remember what I said when you moved in?" Our eyes met and I smiled. "*Mi casa, su casa.*"

"Hmm." He nodded again, but not breaking eye contact.

The look in his eyes made my mouth go dry. "What?"

His lips pulled into a mischievous grin. "I just thought it was funny."

When I wet my lips, he sucked in a breath and looked away, finding something in the distance to hold his attention.

"What was funny?" I asked, turning toward him and resting one elbow on the railing.

He chewed his lip, then met my eyes again. "It was just funny that you would mention that." He moved a little closer to me.

34

"What? *Mi casa, su casa*?" I ran the tip of my tongue across my lower lip, and he jumped as if I'd shocked him.

He inhaled, then squared his shoulders like he was bracing himself for something. "Yeah, that. Because Ethan said exactly the same thing." Before I could reply, he closed the distance between us and kissed me.

As his lips moved gently against mine, I put my hands on his shoulders to steady myself. I hadn't kissed anyone in so damned long, and it was immediately overwhelming. We inched closer together, wrapping our arms around each other as the kiss deepened. His tongue slid under mine, drawing it into his mouth, and my piercing brushed his lip.

He broke the kiss and looked at me, licking his lips as his eyes shifted between my eyes and mouth. "Your tongue's pierced?"

"Maybe it is." I rested my hand on the back of his neck and drew him closer. "You'll just have to confirm that for yourself."

"So I will," he growled, and kissed me again. He quickly found the stud with the tip of his tongue and played with it gently, sending a shiver down my spine.

He leaned me against the railing, pressing his hard cock against mine as his hand drifted down my side and came to rest on my hip. I broke the kiss with a gasp, then dipped my head to kiss his neck. As my hands ran up and down his back, I was desperate for a taste of his skin, but I knew I wouldn't get one tonight. This was the most we could do now, but, damn it, I needed to taste him, smell him, touch him.

"Jesus, I wish I had more time." He panted as I kissed his neck and the underside of his jaw. The hand on my hip moved to the front of my jeans, and he squeezed my cock gently, making my breath catch.

"How much time do you have?" I asked.

He tugged at my belt buckle. "Just enough and not enough."

I lifted my head to kiss him, but faltered when he unbuckled my belt and found my zipper. I was lucky I could stand, let alone speak, but I managed, "Just enough? Not enough? What does that mean?"

He nipped the side of my neck and, as his fingers wrapped around my cock, said, "Not nearly enough time to do everything I want. But *just* enough time for this." In the next heartbeat, he was on his knees with his mouth around my cock.

Jesus, I thought Ethan moved fast. My hands opened and closed in the air where his shoulders had been a second before. When he ran his tongue around the head of my cock a few times, the resulting shudder made my knees buckle, and my hands finally remembered how to keep me upright and grabbed the railing.

I watched in disbelief as Kieran devoured every inch of my cock. Circling with his tongue here, fluttering the tip of it there, stroking with one hand, stroking with both hands.

"Just like that," I slurred, closing my eyes and letting my head fall back. "Fuck yes, just like that..." I could immediately tell that Kieran was the kind of man who decided how fast he made someone come. His lips and tongue knew all the right spots and just how to touch them to send me out of my mind. He could probably make a blowjob last all night if he wanted, or he could make it fast and furious. Tonight, he was going for the latter, and there was nothing I could do but sit back and enjoy it.

A shiver of electricity rippled up my spine, and my hands tightened their grip on the railing as I lost my grip on reality. I managed one gasp for breath, one last helpless whimper, and my vision went white.

"Oh my God," I breathed as my orgasm subsided, as I eased back into the present and tried to stay standing on shaking knees. "That was..." I licked my dry lips. "Incredible."

Kieran stood and cradled my head in both hands as he kissed me deeply.

"When you have more time," I said breathlessly, "I swear to God, I'm going to make this up to you."

"I'm going to hold you to that."

I grinned and kissed him. "Name the time and place."

"Soon, I hope," he whispered. "But for now, I have to go." He kissed me one last time then stepped back, and we straightened our clothes. He dusted off the knees of his tux pants and, without another word, just an exchange of devilish glances, he went back into the house.

I turned around and leaned on the railing, looking out at the glittering skyline. My knees still trembled a little, and I couldn't help but smile to myself.

Maybe this roommate arrangement wouldn't be so bad after all.

Chapter Six

I stayed out on the balcony for a while after Kieran left. When I went inside, Ethan was home. It was all I could do not to gloat when I walked into the kitchen and got a drink.

"Has Kieran already left for work?" he asked.

The corners of my mouth pulled up in spite of my best efforts. "Yeah, he left a while ago." For a moment, neither of us spoke, but I couldn't get the smug grin off my face.

He eyed me warily. "You're all smiles tonight."

I sipped my drink. "I'm allowed to be in a good mood once in a while, aren't I?"

He cocked his head. A second later, enlightenment seemed to hit, and he rolled his eyes. "I don't even want to know."

"Then I won't say a thing." I took a long drink. He gave me another puzzled glance, then shook his head. He'd obviously caught on, but he didn't need to know who it was. He didn't need to know that one of tonight's bartenders at Wilde's had dust on the knees of his tux pants and only I knew why. *Why no, Ethan, you're not the only one who knows how to gloat.*

"Oh, while I'm thinking about it," he said. "Mortgage is due—"

"On the first, just like it always is."

He raised an eyebrow. "I assume I'll have a check from you,

then?"

My good spirits dipped slightly. I was not in the mood to snipe with him about money again tonight. First household bills, now the damned mortgage. "In more than enough time to make the payment, yes. Just like I agreed to do in the beginning."

"Fine. I just want to make sure it has enough time to clear into my account before I make the payment."

"Are we going to go through this every month?" I tightened my fist around my water bottle.

He put his hands up defensively. "I'm just checking."

"You've known me long enough to know I'm not going to fuck around with money."

"I never said you were. It was just a question."

"Sure it was," I muttered. "By the way, Sabrina will be coming by this weekend."

"Oh, good." He smiled. "I haven't seen her in a while."

"She's been busy with midterms. Listen, I..." I hesitated.

He raised an eyebrow. "Hmm?"

I squared my shoulders and forced myself to look him in the eye. "Listen, whatever issues we have going on right now, all this sniping and bullshit, I'd appreciate it if we could keep them out of her sight when she's over."

His lips thinned and his eyes narrowed. "I would never throw this in her face. Any of it."

"That's all I ask."

"Do you really think I would do that?"

There isn't much I'd put past you these days. "No, I'm just—"

"Then there's no need to bring it up, is there?" he snapped.

"Does she even know we're done, or have you sheltered her from that too?"

"She knows," I said through clenched teeth. "She doesn't know about this particular arrangement yet, but she knows we're done. I just don't want us sniping in front of her."

"Give me a little credit, Rhett. My issues are with you, not her." He rolled his eyes and took a drink. "Besides, it isn't like she didn't have front row seats to a great deal of it."

"All the more reason not to let her see any more. Look, she's having a hard time with this. I don't want to make it any worse for her."

"And you think I do?" he growled. "Jesus Christ, Rhett, she's my—" He stopped himself, closing his mouth so fast his teeth snapped together.

We stared at each other. My tongue stud dug into the roof of my mouth and my breath stayed in my lungs. Then he dropped his gaze.

Barely whispering, I said, "She's your what?"

He hesitated. Swallowed hard. "Never mind." A second later, he was gone, his footsteps thudding down the hall in time with my pounding heart.

Leaning against the counter, I sighed and rubbed my forehead. Though the words were unspoken, they resonated through my consciousness.

She's my daughter too.

Biologically, Sabrina was mine, but could I really hold his claim against him? Whatever had happened between us, I couldn't—and wouldn't—deny that Ethan was as much her dad as I was. Sometimes I even wondered if he'd stayed with me for the last few years because of her. Once she'd moved out, he had no reason to stay.

I exhaled hard and ran a hand through my hair. "You really know how to kill a man's good mood, don't you, Ethan?"

Chapter Seven

I was filling my water bottle at the kitchen sink one afternoon when Kieran walked in. My pulse jumped as soon as he stepped into the room. It was the first time we'd seen each other since that incredible encounter on the balcony a few nights ago. Work schedules had kept us out of the house at staggered intervals, but we'd finally managed to be in the same place at the same time.

"Hey." He smiled, but looked a little shy.

"Hey." I turned off the tap and put the top on my water bottle. For a moment, neither of us spoke. Awkward silence fell, and the pounding of my heart made sure I knew just how quiet the room was.

He rested one shoulder against the doorframe. "Just get home from work?"

I leaned against the counter. "Yeah. Well, half an hour or so ago. I was just getting ready to go up and work out."

"Oh." He paused to clear his throat. "I was just, um, going to ask if you could show me a few things." Instantly, his cheeks colored and he coughed, avoiding my eyes. "In the gym. With the weights."

"Perfect timing, then." I gestured at my gym clothes. "I was just heading upstairs."

He smiled. "Great. I'll go change."

I watched him leave the kitchen, then let out a breath. It amazed me that we could be so awkward and clumsy with each other, given how comfortable we were out on the balcony. We could go from a kiss to a blowjob in the space of minutes, but the intricacies of conversation were suddenly too much for us.

And now he wanted me to explain the finer points of weight training, when all I wanted to do was throw him down and fuck him.

For a moment, I stared up at the ceiling, hoping it held an answer or two about how to proceed with this. I knew what I wanted. I hoped he wanted the same. The only question was how to get there. Obviously, I'd become spoiled after a decade with Ethan. We'd long ago made it through all the coy games that always seemed to precede a sexual relationship, and I'd long ago forgotten how much I hated those games. *Damn it, starting over sucks.*

Shaking my head, I left the kitchen and went upstairs to get ready to work out, wondering how I was going to get through my routine without dropping a plate on my foot.

Kieran joined me, and after we'd both stretched—carefully avoiding looking at each other aside from the most surreptitious glances—I said, "So, do you usually do cardio before or after weights?"

He shrugged. "Either way."

"I prefer before." I gestured toward one of the treadmills and got on the other. "You know how to use all the programs?"

He looked at the screen and keypad, then nodded. "Yeah, it's pretty similar to what I've used before."

I set mine to a program of two miles at varying intervals, alternating between two minute jogs and one minute sprints. Kieran went right into a slightly faster pace and stayed at that

43

speed.

"Don't kill yourself," I said after a few minutes. "You'll need plenty of energy after this." He glanced at me with raised eyebrows, and my face burned. I looked straight ahead. "I do high intensity weight training. You'll need your energy for that."

"Oh. Right."

While we ran, we made small talk, keeping it mostly related to working out. Every time we glanced in each other's directions, though, our eyes met and lingered. And every time, the conversation dropped, changing speeds almost in time with my treadmill's intervals.

The treadmills gave us something else to focus on, a reason to shift our eyes. A reason not to ask the question that I hoped he wanted to ask as much as I did. Then the conversation would start again, keeping within the safe confines of everyday life, our respective jobs, and not the fact that I couldn't stop thinking of the incredible blowjob he'd given me the other night.

Sometimes we laughed, but it was always a nervous, forced sound, just like everything we'd said thus far. Oh, how I hated these games, this coy dance of sound and silence: Laughing to avoid talking, talking to avoid silence, silence to avoid going *there.*

When we'd finished our respective runs, I showed him how to do basic one-handed dumbbell curls. His form wasn't bad, but the few mistakes he made gave me an excuse to touch him. Adjusting his posture, turning his wrist to a less strenuous angle, any excuse to put a hand on him, and he didn't object in the slightest.

"So how do you decide how much weight to use?" he asked at one point.

"Depends on how much you need. The whole idea is to push your limits, so it should always be as much as you can take." Our eyes met, and we both swallowed hard. I ignored the way my blood thundered in my ears. "The last rep of every set should be *almost* to the point that you can't do it." At this point, a single rep nearly required more concentration than I could muster.

After a few more basic exercises, I pulled a barbell off the rack.

"It doesn't look like a lot of weight." I gestured at the single ten pound plates on either end of the bar. "But trust me, this is pretty brutal."

He folded his arms across his chest and cocked his head. "With twenty pounds on it?"

"Don't forget the five pound bar."

He rolled his eyes. "Okay, twenty-five pounds."

"Trust me, it's enough. These are called twenty-ones, and they suck."

He laughed. "No pain, no gain, right?"

"Exactly. Now watch." I held the bar, arms straight down and palms facing forward. "Pull it up in a curl, but stop halfway up." I demonstrated, stopping with my forearms parallel to the ground, then let it back down to the starting position, pretending not to notice the way he was watching my arms. "Do seven reps like that. Then bring it up to that halfway point, and do seven reps from there to your chest." I demonstrated a few reps. "And when you're done with that, seven reps from the starting position all the way to your chest. Twenty-one, without stopping." It was considerably less weight than I usually used, but the vague burn in my biceps still made me grimace.

He smirked as I handed him the barbell. "Looks simple enough."

I raised an eyebrow. "I could change them to forty-twos if

you'd like."

He laughed. "Let me do a few sets, then I'll let you know."

I kept my hands just below the center of the bar, not touching it, but ready in case he dropped it. That, and it gave me an excuse to stand this close to him. As he raised it slowly, my gaze flicked back and forth from his biceps to his forearms. Though it wasn't a lot of weight, the ripples of tension beneath his skin were obvious and made my mouth water.

When I glanced up, our eyes met, and he gave me a knowing grin.

With a self-conscious cough, I said, "Like I told you, the whole idea is to push your limits. It should be right at the very threshold of what you can handle." Our eyes met again. I moistened my lips. "What one person can handle might be too much for the next person."

He changed to the second set, going from elbow height to his shoulders. His lips twitched with exertion, but he kept his eyes focused right on mine. "Or not nearly enough for someone else."

I swallowed. "Exactly."

He lowered the weight all the way, starting the set of full curls. A flicker of a grimace tugged at his lips as he started to bring the bar up again. "So how do you figure out how much you can handle?"

"Start with one. Go from there."

"And if one isn't enough?"

I gulped. "Then you try two."

Kieran glanced at the single plate on either end of the bar. He lowered it, set it on the floor and stood. "I'm thinking one isn't quite enough." He stepped over the bar.

The magnitude of his presence made me want to take a

step back, but my desire for him kept my feet planted. "Then I guess you should try two."

He brought his hands up and rested them on my chest just below my collar bones, that light contact pushing the breath out of me. There was no way in hell he didn't feel my heart pounding, and I didn't give a damn if he did. Sliding his hands higher, he neared me inch by inch, but he did so slowly. Agonizingly slowly.

We'd moved so quickly the other night, but now it was the exact opposite. I couldn't put my finger on why. Nerves? Coyness? Savoring the distance? Moving in for this inevitable kiss was like engaging in a staring contest, each waiting for the other to blink.

There was no fear of rejection, not when we'd already covered this much ground. We were going to fuck before this night was over, that much was a foregone conclusion, but still we held back, daring each other with our eyes.

Then I ran the tip of my tongue across my lower lip, and Kieran blinked.

Chapter Eight

From the first second our mouths made contact, the kiss was desperate and breathless. We grasped hair, clothing, skin, whatever we could get our hands on, as long as it got us closer to each other.

Panting, Kieran said, "I could go for a shower right about now."

"Is that an invitation?"

He grinned. "Are you accepting?"

"I am if you promise to kiss me that way again."

He pulled me into a deep, hungry kiss and pressed his hips against me, letting his hard cock brush over mine.

I broke the kiss and growled, "Downstairs. *Now.*"

We managed to make it down the stairs without breaking our necks in spite of stumbling over our own feet and stopping every couple of steps to wind each other up a bit more. Once we were on level ground, I pulled away just long enough to go into my bedroom and grab a couple of condoms and some lube. When I stepped back into the hall, he came out of his room with the very same things in his hand. Our eyes met with a mix of lust and amusement, and I knew the games and coyness were over.

As we went into the bathroom between our bedrooms, it

occurred to me that Ethan could come home at any moment. About the time Kieran took his shirt off, it occurred to me that I really didn't care.

We piled our sweaty gym clothes on the floor. As I reached in to turn the shower on, Kieran's fingers trailed down my upper arm.

"I didn't know you had ink," he whispered.

I glanced over my shoulder, shivering at his featherlight touch as he traced one of my tattoos. "You like tattoos?" I stepped into the shower and gestured for him to join me.

"I fucking love tattoos." He closed the shower door behind him. "And piercings, for that matter."

I put my arms around his waist. "Well, the tattoos are just for decoration." I kissed his neck. Just before my lips found his mouth again, I murmured, "The piercing serves a purpose." He shuddered, which brought his body closer to mine, and kissed me even more passionately. When he went to kiss my neck and shoulder, I ran my fingers over his arms.

"You don't have any ink?" I asked.

"None," he murmured against my collarbone. "Not yet, anyway."

I looked down at his arm and shoulder, biting my lip as I watched my fingers chase streams of water down the grooves of his well-defined muscles. "On one hand, I think you'd look sexy with tattoos. On the other, it would be a crime to cover up arms like this."

"Maybe I should just get them on my back and shoulders, then."

It was my turn to shudder. "My God, if you put ink on those shoulders..." I trailed off, shaking my head.

"What?" he said with a smirk.

I pulled him into a deep kiss. "Put ink on those shoulders and I guarantee I won't be able to keep my hands off of them."

"All the more reason to get them inked, then." He kissed me and ran his hands down my sides. When they came to rest on my hips, he pulled me against him exhaling hard when his hard cock brushed mine. "I have to say," he whispered. "I've been wanting you since the second you answered the door that first day."

I bit my lip as he flicked his tongue across the hollow of my throat. "The feeling's mutual, believe me." Reaching between us, I stroked his cock slowly, barely suppressing a moan of anticipation when I realized just how thick he was.

He breathed in time with my quickening strokes, closing his eyes and holding on to my shoulders for stability.

"Like that?" I whispered, brushing my lips along his jaw.

He nodded, or at least tried to. Even that seemed to require a bit too much concentration for him. His balance wavered, and he took a step back to steady himself. As soon as he did, he gasped as hot water rushed over his shoulders and into the narrow space between his skin and mine.

"I told you the other night that I owed you." I nudged him up against the wall. "I wasn't kidding." Holding onto his hips to steady us both, I went to my knees.

"Oh fuck," he said.

I looked up, running my fingertips down the sides of his thighs. "I haven't even done anything yet."

"I know, but I know how you kiss, so I know you're—"

I made a gentle circle with my tongue on his hipbone. "So you know I'm what?"

He moaned softly as I kissed my way closer to his cock. "I know you'll be fucking incredible at this."

"Then I hope I don't disappoint." I ran my tongue along the underside of his erection. Until that moment, I hadn't realized just how long it had been since I'd tasted cock. Skin was skin, but there was something so deliciously hot about the way a hard cock felt against my tongue. I loved the salt of his skin, the heat of his body, and the twitch and pulse whenever I did something right.

Holding him steady with one hand, I took as much of his cock as I could manage into my mouth, then slowly drew back, running my tongue and stud along the underside. I didn't rely on my piercing to give a blowjob; I just let it emphasize everything my tongue did. An extra hint of stimulation in all the right places and, judging by the way Kieran groaned and trembled, I found all the right places.

His hips mirrored my rhythmic motions, thrusting gently as if to fuck my mouth just a little deeper. He gasped for breath and, as he inched closer to coming, his cock seemed to get even harder, even thicker.

"Oh God, yes, just like that," he moaned. "That's..." His palms hit the wall with a sharp smack, and his back arched. A heartbeat later, he came, and he kept coming. I kept sucking his cock, kept stroking it, and he just kept coming.

Finally, his hand nudged my forehead, and I stopped. Pushing myself to my feet, I wasn't quite balanced when he kissed me. We both stumbled, nearly losing our footing, but I leaned him against the wall again and kept us upright.

He suddenly shifted to one side, and I caught him with my arm, thinking he'd lost his balance, but when he brought his hand up, he had a condom between his fingers. I shivered with anticipation as I took it from him and tore the wrapper. He poured lube in his hand while I put on the condom, and as soon as it was in place, he stroked my cock with the lube. My fingers tangled in his wet hair, and it was all I could do to remember how to kiss him while his hand drove me crazy.

I couldn't wait anymore. I had to be inside him now or I was going to lose my damned mind.

"Turn around," I said.

He did, bracing himself against the wall. A shudder rippled his back and shoulders as I pressed my cock against him. Pushing into him slowly, I released a ragged breath. It had been too long, entirely too long, and I had to fight to stay in control as my cock slid deeper inside him. I wanted to fuck him good and hard, but I was afraid if I moved even a little faster, I'd come, and this was just too damned good to be over just yet.

"Oh God, faster," he moaned.

"Any faster and I'll come," I said through my teeth.

"*Faster.* Fuck me faster."

I held his hips and slowed my strokes, fighting to keep from coming as well as trying to tease him. "I can't hear you, Kieran."

"Faster," he growled, louder now. The need in his voice electrified my senses, and there was no keeping myself in control anymore. I was too long without getting laid, and he just felt too damned good, so I didn't hold back. Grabbing his shoulders, I thrust into him as hard as I could.

"Kieran...that's—" Both exertion and arousal reduced me to short, uneven gasps for breath. "You feel...incredible."

His shoulders rippled beneath my hands, and he took over, pushing himself back and driving me deeper.

When his hips circled one way, then the other, and back again, I lost control.

"Oh Jesus," I groaned, closing my eyes and holding onto him even tighter. "Oh God, I'm—" I came so hard, I lost my balance and slammed both of us up against the wall. He grunted, but kept moving his hips, to draw out my orgasm.

Eventually, my sanity returned and my vision cleared. Steadying myself with one hand on the wall, I withdrew.

I rested my forehead against the back of his neck. "Fuck, that was incredible."

"You're telling me."

I nipped his shoulder. "Hope you're not ready to call it a night yet."

He turned around and kissed me. "I've got plenty left."

"Then why don't we finish in here," I murmured against his lips. "Then go finish this in the bedroom?"

Chapter Nine

After we'd showered, we went into my bedroom and got into bed. Every inch of my body still tingled, and the pleasant ache in my arms and legs had nothing to do with my earlier workout.

"I needed that." I closed my eyes and ran my fingers through my hair.

Kieran looked at me, grinning. "Been a while?"

My cheeks burned. "Was it that obvious?"

He laughed. "Hardly."

"It's been entirely too long, believe me."

With a wink, he said, "Glad I could help." We both fell quiet again, but I got the impression from the way he pursed his lips that he had something on his mind. When he glanced at me, I raised my eyebrows in an unspoken question.

"Okay, I just have to ask." He took a breath and turned onto his side. "About you and Ethan. If you guys aren't together, then—"

"Why do we still live together?"

"Yeah. I mean, I know houses don't sell very fast these days, but..." The lift of his eyebrows finished the question.

I let out a breath. "In theory, we could afford to move out while the place is up for sale, but if either of us tried paying half the mortgage while coughing up rent on an apartment, it would be financially crippling. There's no way we can rent it out for enough money to cover the mortgage, so..." I shrugged. "So we figured we'd keep doing this until the market recovers a bit or we've built up some more equity and can sell it."

"Oh," he said. "That's gotta be a bitch, being stuck together because of something like this."

"You have no idea." I tried to keep the bitterness out of my tone, but didn't quite succeed.

"So what happened? With you and Ethan? I mean, if you don't mind my asking."

"You mean why did we split?"

He nodded.

I sighed. "We just drifted apart, I think. Started wanting different things out of life, stopped wanting each other." I absently stroked his damp hair. "You know a relationship is in trouble when you're fighting so much, even makeup sex takes too much effort."

"Wow, I thought you guys got along pretty well."

Oh, how appearances deceive, my friend. I laughed. "We do, now that we're single."

"Funny what that does to people," he said, chuckling. "I think the best sex my ex and I had was after he helped me move out."

"Ex sex? Damn, that must have been a nice sendoff."

He smiled. "You could say that."

"Beats the hell out of the other options." I laughed. "This is the first time I've been laid in months."

"Are you serious?" He blinked. "How long ago did you guys split?"

I shrugged. "A month ago, maybe a little less?"

"Jesus. That's gotta be a switch after ten years."

"God, you have no idea," I said with an exasperated sigh. "Talk about completely changing your life after getting set in your ways. We were together longer than I've ever been with anyone else. Hell, my marriage didn't last half as long."

"You were married before?"

I nodded. "Four years."

"Decided you were into men after that?"

"Nope. She and I both knew I was bisexual. We were just too young and stupid to be married to each other or anyone else." I shrugged. "So, we split, I dated a few men, a few women, and met Ethan."

He chuckled. "Variety *is* the spice of life."

"Yeah, you could say that." With one hand on the side of his neck, I drew him a little closer and raised my head to kiss just below his jaw. "I'm definitely liking *this* variety."

He released a hiss of breath. "You're not the only one." His hand drifted down my arm, and he kissed my neck as I did the same to his. After a moment, we both raised our heads, and his lips met mine in a long, lazy kiss. I put my arms around him as he ran his fingers through my hair. As the kiss deepened, the tip of his tongue gently slid under mine.

"You know, until tonight," he said, breaking the kiss just enough to allow him to speak, "I'd never actually had a blowjob from someone with a tongue piercing."

"Really?" I let it rattle across my teeth, making him shiver. "I thought you said you liked them."

"I do. Up until now, all I'd ever done was kiss someone with one. I've always wanted a blowjob from someone with a piercing."

I smiled. "Hope it lived up to your expectations."

"Oh, you could say that. In fact..." He reached over me and picked up one of the condoms off the bedside table.

Chapter Ten

One night, about two weeks after Kieran moved in, his shift started in the early evening and Ethan had to work late, so I had my daughter over for dinner. Sabrina lived on the university campus not far from the house, but came by whenever she could get away from her studies.

She leaned on the opposite side of the kitchen island as I made dinner.

"So how is school going?" I asked.

"Getting close to finals," she groaned. "I don't know if I'm going to survive this history class."

"What?" I gave her an incredulous look. "Since when do you have problems with history?"

"It's not the history, it's all the shit the prof wants me to *write* about history. It's one paper after another."

"That, my dear, is college life. Enjoy it."

"Great. Some of the stuff in this class is pretty hard too. Do you think, as I get closer to finals, you can help me with it?"

"Sure." I shrugged. "History's not my best subject, but I'll do what I can."

"Well, it's mostly dealing with the Civil War," she said, a smirk creeping into her expression. "I figured that since you were there—"

"Quiet, you."

She laughed and, as she did, a flicker of something shiny caught my eye.

I dropped my knife. "What the hell is *that*?"

Without moving her mouth any more than she had to, she said, "What's what?"

"You know what. In your mouth."

She pressed her lips together and shrugged.

"Show me." I snapped my fingers. "Come on, I know what I saw."

She shook her head.

I leaned against the counter and tried to look disapproving, but it didn't work. Finally I just laughed. "Okay, just when did you get your tongue pierced, young lady?"

Her cheeks turned red. "A couple months ago," she said, still not moving her mouth very much.

"Show me."

She stuck out her tongue, revealing a silver stud. I thought about asking what possessed her to get it done, but I was afraid she'd tell me. I knew why I'd gotten *mine* pierced, I didn't want to know if my daughter was even thinking about such things. *It's just a fashion thing. It's just a fashion thing. It's just a fashion thing.*

I shook my head and feigned disapproval again. "You're taking proper care of it, I hope?"

She rolled her eyes and said in an exasperated tone, "Yes, Dad, I'm taking care of it."

"I guess I can't really get on your case about it." I picked up the knife and continued cutting vegetables. "Though I thought I told you no piercings until you were thirty-five."

"You got yours when you were thirty."

"Yes, thirty. Which is a far cry from eighteen, kiddo."

"Uh-huh. And weren't you eighteen when you got your first—"

"*No. Tattoos.*"

She raised an eyebrow. "Do you regret yours?"

"No."

"Think it was worth it?"

I pursed my lips. "Yes."

With a smug grin, she said, "And can you legally stop me from getting one?"

I smirked. "Okay, you got me. You're an adult, you can go graffiti yourself if you really want to."

"Like I need your permission." She snorted.

"One thing, though." I gave her the sternest look I could muster.

"Let me guess. Don't tell Mom?"

"Yeah, right." I rolled my eyes. "What's she going to do? Ground us both?"

Sabrina laughed. "Okay, point taken."

"No, my one condition, or rather a request, since I can't actually stop you either way, and I'm dead serious about this: I want to take you to get it done."

Her jaw dropped. "Seriously?"

I nodded. "Now don't think this is some trendy father-daughter bonding bullshit," I said. "I'd rather you waited until you were older, but if you're going to get a tattoo, I want to make sure you're getting it done at a clean, safe place."

"So I can't have it done in someone's basement with—"

"No." We both laughed, then I said, "That, and I want to be

there so that when it gets really, really painful, I can rub it in that I told you so."

"You would, too."

"Yes, I would. Damn, your mother is going to be pissed the first time she sees you with a piercing and a tattoo. What kind of bad influence am I?"

"So if I said I had a girlfriend, you think she'd get upset?"

My eyebrows jumped and the knife stopped in midair. "You what?"

"Dad! Jesus H. Christ." She clicked her tongue. "I don't even have a boyfriend." She laughed. "So, when you take me to get my tattoo, are you also paying for it?"

I resumed cutting. "I guess that brings me to my next question."

"Which is?"

"Just what the fuck have you been smoking since you moved out of this house?"

"Oh please, I'm just trying to be like my daddy." She batted her eyes.

"Yeah, well, your daddy paid for his own tattoos and piercing, and so will you."

She started to speak, but then a door down the hall opened and closed. The hairs on the back of my neck stood on end. I hadn't even thought about having Sabrina meet my roommate, but suddenly I was faced with her meeting my—and Ethan's—lover. *Oh God, this is going to be awkward.*

Sabrina cocked her head. "I thought you said Ethan was out."

"He is."

As if on cue, Kieran walked in, and I thought I would have to pick my daughter's jaw up off the floor. I couldn't blame her.

He was dressed for work, though his bowtie still hung untied around his neck.

"Kieran, this is my daughter Sabrina," I said.

"Nice to meet you," he said.

"Likewise," she said as they shook hands.

Then he turned and pulled a bottle of water out of the refrigerator. To me, he said, "I'm off to work, but I have some clothes in the dryer. They weren't done yet, but I'll take them out when I get home."

I made a dismissive sweep with one hand. "Don't worry about it."

He glanced at his watch. "Well, I'd better run. Shift starts in half an hour." To Sabrina, he said, "Nice meeting you."

"You too." She sounded almost dazed.

Kieran and I exchanged glances, keeping our expressions neutral. Then he left. Sabrina watched him walk out, and I could tell by the way she was craning her neck that she was watching him in ways no father wanted to see his daughter watch any man.

"Sabrina," I said in a loud whisper.

"What?" She put her hands up and widened her eyes. "I wasn't—"

"Yes, you were," I said in a half-heartedly disapproving growl, gesturing at her with a spatula. "He's not your type."

She sighed theatrically. "Damn it, he's gay, isn't he?"

I laughed. "That, and he's too old for you."

"What? Is he nineteen?"

"Twenty-five. But he's off limits, so back off." Something about the two of them meeting at all unsettled me. Not that I was concerned about them hooking up. As far as I could tell,

Kieran wasn't interested in women. Even if he was, he'd probably be afraid I'd kill him if he so much as looked at my daughter, which I would have.

Having them meet just seemed...strange.

Sabrina glanced at the doorway through which Kieran had just disappeared. "So, what is he doing here? Besides his laundry?" She gave me a suspicious look.

"He's renting the spare bedroom. Helping us make some headway on the mortgage so we can sell the place."

Her shoulders slumped a little and her humor evaporated. "So you guys really are going to sell it?"

I nodded. "Eventually."

"And things with you and Ethan," she said quietly. "They're really, you know..."

"Over?"

She flinched. "Yeah."

I sighed and set the knife down, leaning against the island. "Yeah, it's over. We're just living together until we've gained enough equity in the house to sell it without taking a hit."

Resting her elbows on the counter, she chewed her thumbnail. She suddenly looked less like my man-watching tongue-pierced eighteen year-old and more like the little girl who I had to gently explain "divorce" to a lifetime ago. "Have you guys at least tried to work things out?" she asked.

I swallowed hard. "We've been trying to work it out for a long time, baby. You know that. There just comes a point when people have to go their separate ways."

"Wow. I just..." She shook her head. "I guess I thought you guys would..."

"I know," I whispered. "Me too."

She glanced at the doorway again, then looked at me with

63

one eyebrow raised. "So have you met anyone else yet?"

"No, I haven't."

"What about Kieran?"

I laughed, hoping to hide any color that showed up in my cheeks. "Remember how I said he's a little old for you?"

"He's a little young for you?"

"Exactly."

"You could always come by the dorms and I'll see if I can hook you up," she said, obviously trying not to laugh. "Put up a sign that says, *My bisexual dad—*"

"Sabrina!" My cheeks were on fire. "Jesus Christ."

She laughed. "Okay, fine, just guys, then."

"Watch it, or I'll make sure the tattoo artist customizes your design to *my* specs."

"Yeah." She laughed. "And it'll probably say *'Rhett Solomon's Daughter, Do Not Touch'.*"

"Exactly. So watch yourself." After a moment, I said, "Are you okay with this? I mean, with Ethan and me…"

She chewed her lip and shrugged halfheartedly. "Not much I can say about it, is there?"

"Well, yeah, but you're part of the family too. He's been in the picture for a long time."

She was quiet for a long moment. "Would it bother you if I stayed in touch with him?"

I winced. Not because she wanted to stay in touch with him, but it was just one more "yes, this is really happening" moment, another confirmation that this was ending. Ethan had been a part of Sabrina's life since she was eight. I wouldn't begrudge her the need to keep in contact with him any more than I'd hold it against him.

"Dad?"

"Sorry. Of course, I wouldn't keep you from staying in touch with him." I gave her what I hoped was a reassuring smile.

She smiled back, but it didn't quite make it to her eyes.

Chapter Eleven

Later that evening, not long after Sabrina left, I was out on the balcony when the front door opened. Thinking she must have forgotten something, I stepped back inside, but it wasn't Sabrina.

"You're home early," I said.

Kieran shrugged, loosening his bowtie. "I was just working a half shift. They had a show tonight, so they needed a few extras behind the bar."

"A show?" I leaned against the sofa, hooking my thumbs in my pockets. "I'm told Wilde's has some pretty crazy shows."

He whistled. "You could say that. These guys would've put the Chippendales to shame, let me tell you."

"God damn," I said. "And why didn't you tell me about this in advance? So I could go check it out?"

"Well, I could have." With a shrug and a devilish grin, he started toward me. "But then you might have seen something you liked." He put his hands on my waist and dipped his head to kiss my neck.

"Mm-hmm." I closed my eyes as he nipped just above my collar. "And why would that be a bad thing?"

He flicked his tongue across my skin. "Because then I couldn't have you for myself tonight."

"I would have shared. It's not like I'm not sharing you now."

He laughed softly and came up to kiss my mouth. "I'm not averse to sharing a man. I can even be persuaded into a threesome, if they're hot enough." His tongue slid between my lips and his hands untucked my shirt. "But I just wanted you tonight."

"I'm flattered," I said into his kiss.

"And I'm horny." He pressed his hips against mine to let me know just how true that statement was. "I could really use a shower first, but I've been wound up all damned night."

I smiled. "Then maybe I should help you take care of that."

"I was hoping you would," he murmured against my lips.

"I can certainly try."

He kissed me one more time, then freed himself from my arms. "Give me about ten minutes to grab a shower."

I nodded toward my bedroom. "You know where to find me."

While he took a shower, I went into my room and stripped out of my clothes. Lying on my bed, I closed my eyes and listened to the running water in the next room. Between the memories of showering with him, my own imagination about what he was doing now and my anticipation of having him afterward, I was almost painfully hard.

Minutes later, the shower cut off, and my heart sped up. Faster when the bathroom door opened. Even faster when the floor creaked in the hall and my bedroom doorknob turned.

He stepped into my room wearing only a towel around his waist, and as soon as the door was closed, the towel fell away.

I grinned as he joined me in bed. "I see you've been thinking impure thoughts," I said, running a single fingertip along his fully erect cock.

He did the same to my own hard-on. "Obviously I wasn't the only one."

I ran my fingers through his wet hair and kissed him. Once his tongue met mine, there was no further banter. It was neither needed nor possible, because all I knew was how much I wanted him. I hadn't even realized just how horny I was until he was in my bed. It had only been a few days, since the last time we'd slept together, but I needed him. Badly.

I rolled him onto his back. Kissing his neck, his collarbone, his shoulder, I couldn't get enough of the taste of his skin. The taste of *him*. Circling my tongue around his nipple, I watched his face, and every time he wetted his lips and screwed his eyes shut, I inched a little closer to madness.

Holding myself up on trembling arms—*What's the matter with me? I've barely touched him and I'm losing my mind*—I worked my way down his chest and abs. My lips followed the trail of sparse, dark hair from below his navel, my breath catching every time his skin quivered at my touch.

"Oh my God," he groaned, combing his fingers through my hair as I ran both tongue and stud down the side of his cock. He shuddered when I took as much as I could into my mouth. "Holy...that feels amazing..."

Driven by his moans, I stroked and sucked him like my life depended on it, finding just the right speed and all the right spots to send him into orbit. My own cock twitched when his did, aching as his seemed to get thicker and harder.

"Oh fuck, Rhett, you're gonna make me come, that's..." His entire body jerked and he gasped for breath. "Not yet, I want to—" He gasped again, his hips lifting off the bed, and I stroked him faster while I circled the head of his cock with my tongue. "Oh God, I want—" He moaned and arched his back. "Fuck, fuck, don't—" His cock pulsed against my lips and tongue.

"Don't stop, don't fucking stop..."

With every gasp and tremor, his voice became progressively louder and the words more slurred and profane until he released a breathless, helpless cry, and came.

I didn't waste any time. As soon as he let me know he wanted me to stop, I sat up and reached for the drawer beside the bed, letting him catch his breath while I found a condom.

"Your mouth is fucking incredible," he said, still slurring a little.

I tore the wrapper, then leaned down to kiss him lightly. "You're not half bad yourself."

He grinned. "You didn't complain."

"No, I definitely didn't." Rolling the condom on with shaking hands, I was ready to come just from anticipation. I had no idea how the hell I was even going to hold myself up, not when I was this close to going out of my mind.

Kieran put his hands over mine, stilling them, and sat up. Kissing me gently, he nudged my hands aside and rolled the condom on the rest of the way.

He grinned. "You're shaking."

"What can I say?" I whispered, holding both sides of his neck and kissing him again. "You've got me that turned on."

"Well, if it's my fault—" he leaned away to get the bottle of lube, "—then I should do something about it, shouldn't I?" With the bottle in hand, he put his arms around me and kissed me while he used his body weight to guide me down onto my back. His lips went to my neck and shoulder, every gentle kiss making me tremble that much more.

I was just about to beg him not to tease me, to just let me fuck him before I went completely out of my mind, when he sat up. He poured some lube into his hand and closed the top of the bottle, leaving it well within reach on the bed.

Biting my lip, I closed my eyes and sucked in a breath as he sat over me. When he lowered himself onto my cock, I put my hands on his hips just so I could touch him, so I had something to hold onto that was still connected to reality.

He was completely in control of everything—how deep, how fast—and he took full advantage of it. Every time I adapted to one speed, he changed it. Faster, until I was right on the brink, then slow, until I'd almost returned to terra firma, then right back to riding me as fast as he could. Just like he did whenever he went down on me, he kept me right where he wanted me, denying me a release from the deliciously painful tension that built with every incredible thrust.

"Harder, Kieran," I pleaded, thrusting up to meet him. "Jesus fucking Christ, that's perfect."

He brought me right to the edge again, then slowed down, but this time he cursed under his breath.

"You okay?" I asked.

"Yeah," he said, panting and cursing again. "Knees are getting tired."

"Let me get behind you, then."

"That I can do." He smiled and leaned down to kiss me.

In spite of shaking arms and legs, we managed to change positions. I knelt behind him, put on some more lube and slid back into him.

Finally back in control, I held on to his hips and *lost* control. As my speed increased, so too did my voice. I was always vocal, but not like this. Never like this. Then again, I wasn't usually this turned on, this desperate, this overwhelmed by the sheer need to be inside someone and fuck him faster and harder and—

"Oh God, oh God, Kieran, that's…" I gasped, then released a moan that became a roar, and the world went white.

When the aftershocks subsided, I held onto him for balance, letting my vision clear and breath return. It took every bit of energy and focus I had left to get the condom off and disposed of, then I fell into bed beside him, panting and dizzy.

"Wow," I said.

He wiped his forehead and laughed. "I'm going to need another shower after that."

I smiled. "Mind if I join you?"

"Not at all."

"Sweet." I ran a hand through my sweaty hair. "Just give me a minute or two."

"Tell me about it," he said, almost slurring. He rested his head on my shoulder, and the room fell silent except for our rapid breathing.

Then, from upstairs, the telltale creak of floorboards accommodating weight reverberated down the walls. We both looked up.

Staring at the ceiling, I said, "I guess Ethan's home." My eyes tracked the sound as he moved around upstairs, following his footsteps as if I could see him.

"Think he heard us?"

"Yeah, it's a pretty safe bet." I cringed inwardly. After a moment, though, I couldn't help but chuckle. "Well, it's not like I haven't heard you guys."

Kieran laughed. "Fair enough. I guess turnabout's fair play."

Stroking his hair, I kept looking at the ceiling, an amused grin pulling at my lips "Yeah, I guess it is."

Chapter Twelve

When Ethan shuffled into the kitchen the next day, he looked like hell—exhausted, pale, desperate for some caffeine. He looked for all the world like someone who couldn't sleep because he was listening to everyone else in the house having sex. *My, my, how does that shoe feel on the other foot, Mr. Mallory?*

I grinned behind my coffee cup. "Morning."

"Morning," he grumbled, but didn't look at me.

"You okay?" I asked. "You don't look like you slept very well."

He said nothing, didn't even look at me as he picked up the coffee pot. I watched him pour a cup and, to my surprise, his hand was a little unsteady.

My amusement faded. I knew what annoyed Ethan was like, and I knew what annoyed, sleep-deprived Ethan was like. This was neither. No dirty looks, no snide comments. The shaking hand.

Setting my coffee cup down, I said, "You okay?"

He nodded slowly and looked at the floor. I pressed my tongue stud against the roof of my mouth, unnerved by his silence and unsure how to proceed. As his boyfriend or even his friend, I'd have pressed, but I wasn't sure if it was my place to do that anymore. So much for things being simpler since we'd split up. It seemed to be more complicated now that we'd simplified things.

He took a sip of coffee and rolled it around in his mouth for a moment. Swallowing it, he finally looked at me. "I've got a job interview coming up."

"Really? I didn't realize you'd gotten any calls." Not that he owed me an explanation, but it was strange to have these conversations at such a distance now. When things like this came as a surprise.

He nodded. "Yeah. A few."

"Well, good luck."

"Thanks," he murmured. "The reason I'm mentioning it is, um..." He paused. "I'll be out of town. For a few days."

I swallowed. "Toronto?"

He nodded, and something in my chest dropped.

"Oh. Wow. Um, when are you going?"

"End of the month."

I cleared my throat. "Do, um, do you think you'll get it?"

"They liked my phone interviews. If they're willing to fly me out there for a face-to-face, I'd say the odds in my favor." He smiled, but it wasn't as enthusiastic as I'd have expected. Maybe he was just nervous about interviewing with them.

"That's—" I hesitated. "That's great."

He dropped his gaze. "Yeah. So, anyway, I just wanted to give you a heads up."

"If you get it, when would you be moving?"

"Probably not long after," he said quietly. "A few weeks, at most. They need someone in that job fairly quickly, and at least the immigration crap won't be such a headache since I'm still a citizen."

"Good, good." I tried to force enthusiasm that just refused to be forced. "It's, um, I guess it's a pretty good job, then?"

"It's not bad." He watched his thumb trace the edge of the counter. "Pay's about the same, when you factor in the exchange rate. Same kind of work. It's mostly a..." He trailed off.

I swallowed. "Change of scenery?"

Our eyes met briefly, then his darted away. "Yeah."

It shouldn't have hit me in the gut, but it did. "Guess I can't blame you. Change of scenery, all of that." *And Portland is sounding better and better by the minute.*

We stood in uncomfortable silence for a moment. Then his coffee cup made a gentle clank as he set it in the sink. "Anyway, I just wanted to let you know. I should, um, I should go get ready for work."

I didn't speak. He stared at the floor between us and took a breath. I thought he was going to speak and caught myself bracing for whatever he still had to say, but instead he exhaled and walked out of the kitchen.

Rubbing my eyes, I tried not to groan. At every possible opportunity, we found another barrier to put up between us. Walls. Ceilings. A few thousand miles. An international border. Kieran. Nail after nail in this coffin, and each one took my breath away.

My heart sank deeper as I realized we were really getting close to the end. The relationship was over, the love was gone, but there were a few nails left to be driven, and we were getting closer to the day when they would be.

I shook my head and let out the breath I didn't know I was holding. Obviously, I was just ready for this whole process, this slow, painful removal of a bandage, to be over. Part of me hoped that when I came home from work that very night, Ethan and his things would be long gone and bound for Toronto.

But I knew he would still be here.

Long gone, but still here.

Chapter Thirteen

When I pulled in the driveway that evening, Ethan was far from gone. In fact, he and my daughter were in front of the garage playing basketball. They stepped aside, waiting until I was in the garage to resume their game.

"So who's winning?" I asked.

Sabrina sank a spectacular shot that was nothing but net and smirked at Ethan. "I'm ahead by three points."

"The hell you are." He snorted. "You're ahead by two."

She rolled her eyes. "We're going to have to start keeping score on paper if you can't remember, old man."

"Watch it." His grin completely undermined the threat in his tone. She shot him a good-natured glare, then rested the ball on her hip and hugged me with her free arm.

"Well, whenever you're done with the game, we can head out," I said. We'd planned to go out to dinner, then I was taking her grocery shopping to make sure her dorm was well-stocked with halfway decent food. No child of mine was living off day-old pizza and Doritos for four years.

Sabrina looked at her watch and shrugged. "Four more points and I win. Plenty of time for that."

I watched them shooting hoops and talking trash, just like they always did. And just as Sabrina predicted, it wasn't long before she had her four points, though Ethan did give her a run for her money, scoring three points along the way.

Ethan shook his head. "Okay, you win *this* time."

"I win every time."

"She's got you there," I said.

He let out a huff of breath and shook his head. Wiping sweat from his brow, he said, "You know, if this were a regulation game—"

"Don't they have age limits for regulation games?" she said.

I snorted with laughter.

Ethan rolled his eyes. "Mouthy kid," he muttered, trying not to chuckle.

"She thinks she's all grown up." I gave an apologetic shrug. "Doesn't respect her elders anymore."

"Fuck you." Ethan laughed.

"And how about this rebelliousness?" I gestured at Sabrina. "Did she show you her latest, um, 'accessory'?"

Ethan eyed her. "No, I can't say she did."

To my daughter, I said, "Come on. Show him."

"Do I have to?" She tried to look petulant, but cracked a smile.

"Yes," Ethan and I said in unison.

Rolling her eyes, she stuck out her tongue.

Ethan's jaw dropped. "When the hell did you get that thing?"

"You don't like it?" She batted her eyes.

He tried to look stern. "I'm not sure you're quite old enough for things like that."

She clicked her tongue and rolled her eyes again. "Great, now *both* of my *dads* disapprove."

At that, all three of us froze, eyes flicking back and forth.

Ethan coughed, then forced a laugh. "Well, I wouldn't say I disapprove, but…" The damage was done and the awkwardness held fast. For a few minutes, we'd managed to keep this charade of a family going, pretending that this wasn't just an echo of times that would soon be a distant memory, but reality had made itself known and wouldn't be forgotten.

I shifted my weight and looked at Sabrina. "Why don't I go change clothes, and we can get going before it gets too late?"

"Sure." She didn't look at either of us. Then she cleared her throat and tossed the basketball to Ethan, who reacted just in time to catch it. "We have time to play for a few more points."

"As long as you don't cheat this time," Ethan said with a smile that looked marginally more genuine. As they went back to their game, I ducked into the house and went into my bedroom to get dressed.

More than ever, I understood why people sometimes stayed together for their kids. Even though mine was an adult now, she couldn't hide the fact that it tore her up to watch us go our separate ways, and that was killing me. Divorcing her mother when Sabrina was barely four years old was difficult enough, but now she was old enough to know what was going on. It was inevitable, it was for the best, but it wasn't easy.

The more distance Ethan and I put between us, the more aware I was that this wasn't just a simple breakup. The three of us had been as much a family as my ex-wife, daughter and I had been. And like that family, this one had to be split up.

With my heart in my throat, I picked up my jacket and wallet and headed back out to the garage.

"Ready to go?" I said.

"Yeah," she said. "Be right there."

As I got in the car, I watched them in the rearview. I couldn't hear them, but I got the feeling he was offering some kind of reassurance. His hand was on her shoulder, his eyebrows raised and his other hand gesturing almost apologetically as he spoke. She nodded now and again, dropping her gaze a few times only to raise it when he, as far as I could tell, asked her to.

Finally, he smiled at her and she returned it, if tentatively.

My heart fell to my feet when he hugged her and his eyes shifted skyward, then closed as he took a breath. He looked for all the world like he was struggling to keep his composure.

A moment later, they separated, and she got into the car. He walked past the driver's side and into the house without looking back.

Neither Sabrina nor I spoke for a few minutes, not until we were several blocks away from the house.

"You doing okay?" I asked.

She nodded, but said nothing as she stared out the passenger side window.

"You sure?"

"Yeah. It's just, you know..." She hesitated. "It's weird."

"I know what you mean." We continued in silence for a while. I rolled my piercing back and forth across the roof of my mouth, wondering if I should bring up the subject of Ethan leaving the area. For all I knew, he may have already told her. Or maybe he was waiting until he knew for sure. Either way, if he got a job offer, he'd be moving fairly soon, and I wanted her to have some time to accept it.

I took a breath. "Has Ethan told you he's looking for another job?"

"No. I thought he liked where he's working now."

I chewed the inside of my cheek. "Listen, I wasn't going to say anything until he found out for sure, but..." I paused. "He's looking at some jobs that are, well, out of the area."

"Out of the area?" There was a note of panic in her voice that made me cringe, especially as I went on.

"He might be moving back to Toronto."

She released a breath. "Toronto?"

"Yeah," I said as I pulled to a stop at a red light. "He wants to be closer to—" I paused again.

"To his family?" Bitterness replaced panic.

"To the rest of his family, yes."

A full minute passed. Sabrina stared out her window, her expression unreadable from what little I could see in the side mirror. Judging by the slow side to side movement of her jaw, she'd developed my habit with her piercing when she was thinking.

"If he goes to Toronto—" She bit her lip, "—you won't mind if I go visit him, will you?"

Relief swept over me. She'd always been able to cope with things better than anyone twice her age, so it shouldn't have surprised me that she wasn't fighting circumstances that were beyond her control. She always seemed to accept when she couldn't change something, and forced herself to adapt, no matter how hard it was.

"No, no, of course I don't mind."

"Are you sure?"

"Absolutely." The light turned green, and I pulled forward. Glancing at her, I said, "In fact, you two work out the details, I'll buy the ticket."

She finally looked at me. "Seriously?"

I nodded. Then I gave her a stern look. "But that's only

while you're still in college. Once you graduate and get a respectable job, you're buying your own tickets."

"So if I drag out my school until I'm thirty—"

"Four years. No more."

She laughed. "What if I go to graduate school?"

"Don't push your luck."

She smiled. "Thanks, Dad."

"You're welcome, baby. I told you I won't keep you from him. He's—" I stopped myself.

"He's what?"

I swallowed hard, remembering Ethan's expression when he hugged her. "He's your dad too."

Chapter Fourteen

The following night, my friend Dale invited me out for a couple of beers at a new microbrew place in Fremont. Given that Kieran had the night off and Ethan was also home, I didn't hesitate to join Dale as far across town as I could get.

My mind, however, stayed firmly planted in the house on Capitol Hill.

"Dude, Rhett, you okay?" Dale asked as he brought our second round to the table.

"Yeah, yeah, I'm fine." I picked up my pint glass. "Just..."

"Distracted, by the looks of it. What's up?"

Letting out a breath, I set down my glass. "Things with Ethan are a bit more complicated now."

"Complicated?" Dale eyed me. "You've broken up. It doesn't get much more complicated than that. I mean unless—" His eyes suddenly widened, and he sucked in a breath.

I raised my eyebrows. "Unless?"

He put his hand on his chest and gasped in mock surprise. "You knocked him up, didn't you?"

I burst out laughing. "Yeah, Dale, that's it."

He chuckled. "Okay, so what's really going on? I can't see how things could be more complicated unless the two of you are back together." He gave me a pointed look. "Which you're not, I hope."

"Why? Come on, Dale, he's not a bad guy."

He rolled his eyes and sighed. "No, but you were miserable with him."

I nodded. "Yeah, and I'm still miserable with him."

"Oh Jesus fucking Christ, Rhett." He threw up his hands. "You did get back together with him, didn't you?"

"Not quite. We're definitely not together, but we do live together."

"I thought he moved out."

"He was going to. Until we talked to a realtor and the bank and realized that with the market right now, we stand to take a pretty serious hit if we sell the house. And if we both move out, even if we rent it out, we'll be coughing up money left and right to pay rent on our own places, and—" I shook my head. "Anyway, basically, we're stuck with the house for a while. So, we're both staying there until either the market improves or we have some decent equity."

"Except it could take years to build up that kind of equity."

"Right." I ran my fingers around the rim of my glass, watching them to avoid Dale's scrutiny. "Which is why we've taken a roommate to speed up the process a little." I chanced a look at him. "And having a roommate is making things a bit more complicated."

"A roommate?" He shrugged. "So what? How the hell is that making things more complicated with Ethan?"

Avoiding Dale's eyes, I watched my fingers on my glass. "Let's put it this way, our roommate is hot." I paused and cleared my throat. "Like, 'he's a bartender at Wilde's' hot."

"No fucking way. You're living with one of those guys?" He gave a wistful sigh. "Rhett Solomon, do tell me you're banging the living hell out of—" His eyes widened. "*Oh.*"

"Yeah, I am." I rested my elbows on the table, closed my eyes, and rubbed the back of my neck. "I am, and so is Ethan."

"That lucky bastard," Dale muttered.

I looked up. "What?"

"Nothing." He gestured for me to continue. "Anyway, so you're all living together, and you're all sleeping together—"

"Well, Ethan and I aren't sleeping together, but I'm pretty sure he heard us the other night. Since he'd gloated a bit the night I heard them—"

"My God, what I wouldn't do to spend a night in that house." Dale shivered. "It's like audio porn from all directions."

I laughed. "Yeah, aside from all the awkwardness of knowing it's your ex-boyfriend and your lover in the next room."

He gestured dismissively. "Details."

"*Anyway*, it's made things a bit awkward. I heard them one night, and he knew it." I took a drink and muttered, "Gloating motherfucker."

"Did he know you were doing the guy too?"

I shook my head. "I wasn't at the time. But now I am, so the other night, we got a bit loud—"

"Unintentionally, of course."

"Of course." I smirked. "Okay, it really was unintentional, because I didn't know Ethan was home. But, once I figured it out, it was, shall we say, amusing."

"No kidding." Dale snorted with laughter. "Turnabout's fair play, I think."

"Exactly what Kieran said, ironically." I laughed.

"Kieran?" Dale said. "Damn, even his name is sexy."

"You should see him." I winked. "So, the next morning, I'm

The Distance Between Us

all ready to turn the tables a little, not that ex-boyfriends would *ever* be so petty to each other, but then..." My smile fell and something in my chest sank. I sighed and rubbed my forehead with two fingers. "Ethan was in a mood. And then he tells me he's got this job interview coming up in Toronto, and I..." I shook my head.

"So, what?" Dale gestured with his drink. "You're worried he's going to take off to Toronto and leave you with the house and its gorgeous contents?"

I exhaled heavily. "That's what I was worried about when he first told me he was thinking of moving back. He was getting out, I was saddled with the house and, even though he'd still be paying, I'd be stuck."

"Understandable."

"But when he told me he had this interview..." I searched for the right words, making a frustrated gesture as I sat back in my chair. "It just, it hit me right in the gut, and I don't know why."

"Rhett, think about it." He looked at me as if I'd lost my mind. "It makes perfect sense."

"It does?"

"Well, yeah. My God, you've been with him for, how long?"

I shrugged with one shoulder. "Ten years and some change."

"So, a pretty good chunk of your life." He pursed his lips. "I mean, even at your age, ten years—"

"Watch it." I tried and failed not to laugh.

He snickered. "Anyway, it's a pretty good chunk of your life, and now it's ending. Of course you're going to have a hard time with it."

"But it's already ended." I rubbed the back of my neck. "It

85

ended a while ago."

He shook his head. "No, you guys called it off. You put in your notice, gave your resignation to HR, but as long as you boys both live in that house, you're still working for the Ethan and Rhett Company."

I chuckled and rolled my eyes. "Dale, you have such a way with words."

"I'm serious, though. You're probably just freaking out because it's ending, but it hasn't ended yet."

I took a long drink, letting what he'd said settle into my mind for a moment. "You're probably right. I don't know, it just feels weird. I mean, I want it to be over. I want it over fucking *yesterday*. But when he told me he was going to Toronto, that he actually had an interview and a job situation that looks promising..." I pressed my tongue stud into the roof of my mouth, not even sure what I was trying to say let alone how to say it.

"Do you want him to stay?"

"No!" I said quickly. "Good God, no."

He eyed me. "Sure about that?"

I shifted uncomfortably. "Of course. I've been ready for him to leave for a long time."

Skepticism lifted his eyebrow. "So then what are you worried about? If you know you're just anxious for him to leave, why try to analyze it further than that?"

I ran my tongue stud across my teeth and stared into my drink. He was right. I shouldn't have been this hung up on Ethan moving on; I should have been busy moving on from Ethan.

"You miss him, don't you?" Dale said.

"Miss him?" I rolled my eyes. "Please. He has to leave before missing him becomes an issue."

Dale gave me a knowing look. "Does he?"

"What do you mean?"

"I think you already miss him."

I shook my head. "No, no, definitely not. I just want it over."

"And you don't want to listen to him fucking your boytoy," he said with a smirk.

I laughed. "Yeah, that would be nice too."

Chapter Fifteen

When I pulled in the driveway, every window in the house was dark, so I assumed everyone was asleep. Ethan's car was in the garage and Kieran's was parked out by the curb, so they were home, but most likely asleep.

No doubt in the same damned bed, I thought, shoving the gearshift into park.

As I took the stairs up from the garage, a faint flicker caught my attention along with music and unfamiliar voices. One of them must have been watching a movie, I guessed. Or both of them. Together.

My suspicion was confirmed as I neared the living room and the light became brighter and the sounds clearer. Some of the dialogue was audible now and vaguely registered in my memory, but I couldn't place the title of the movie.

Then, as I stealthily walked through the living room, trying not to disturb whoever was watching the film, movement caught my eye. Movement that wasn't on the television screen. I did a double-take and my jaw went slack as I stared in disbelief.

Evidently oblivious to my presence, Ethan sat on the couch and Kieran knelt in front of him, his back to me and his head bobbing rhythmically over Ethan's lap.

Completely stunned, I couldn't tear my eyes away. I couldn't decide whether or not I should be shocked or jealous, but one thing was for sure: It was hot. It was *damned* hot.

If Kieran knew I was there, he gave no indication.

Ethan, however, lifted his head and saw me.

He looked right at me and grinned as he picked up the remote and clicked off the television, rendering the room completely silent except for my heartbeat, Ethan's ragged breathing and Kieran's occasional enthusiastic murmur. A few slender beams of stark white light spilled in from the streetlights, offering vague, glowing outlines of the scene on the couch.

Minimal light and dark shadows emphasized every nuance of Ethan's face, from the furrows between his eyebrows to the tightness of his lips. He closed his eyes and let his head fall back, licking his lips slowly. His fingers contrasted sharply with Kieran's dark hair, and my scalp tingled just thinking about what it was like to have his fingers run through my hair like that while I sucked his cock.

"Oh God, yes," Ethan groaned, just loud enough for me to hear. "That's perfect, Kieran." He bit his lip, his back arching off the couch. Every tremor lifted his spine a little higher, and he closed his eyes and gasped for breath.

Kieran stopped and said something, something I couldn't quite understand, and Ethan's eyes flew open, staring unseeing at the ceiling as his lips formed a silent "oh fuck..." before Kieran resumed his perfect, deliberate rhythm. Ethan whimpered softly, a violent tremor rippling through him.

I couldn't watch anymore. Without making a sound, I hurried down the hall, shutting my bedroom door as quietly as I could. Then I leaned against it, closing my eyes and trying to catch my breath.

I was so turned on I couldn't see straight. Any embarrassment or jealousy I might have had because of walking in on them barely registered, because watching Kieran go down on Ethan was the hottest thing I'd ever seen.

A low groan from down the hall made my breath catch.

"Jesus, Kieran, that's—" His words were slurred and his voice barely audible through the door; this wasn't a sound he made for my benefit or frustration. He wasn't taunting me. He'd probably forgotten I existed at all, because Kieran was driving him wild. Giving a little, sending him close to the edge, then pulling back, letting him calm down just enough to keep him from coming, then giving a little more.

With trembling hands, I unfastened my belt and zipper. I didn't bother moving away from the door. Any farther away and I wouldn't be able to hear him anymore. That, and I couldn't be sure my legs would stay under me without the door to hold me up.

Every time Ethan moaned, every time his voice painted a picture in my mind of his face as he slowly came unraveled at the hands and mouth of Kieran, I inched a little closer to madness. I was barely even aware of my own hand touching my cock, not with Ethan's crescendoing voice and the images in my head of his eyes screwed shut, his lips parted, and his body shaking with the force of impending release. Kieran sent Ethan higher, and Ethan in turn sent me higher.

Ethan was almost silent now except for the occasional gasp, but I swore I could feel him. His building tension, his pounding heart, that deliciously unbearable heartbeat of near panic just before he came, and when he did, the air around me seemed to shudder with the power of his release. His breathless whimper drowned in the sound of my whispered cry, the force of my own orgasm nearly driving me to my knees.

By the time my vision cleared and the room stopped spinning, the low murmur of voices hummed in the air. They were moving, taking uneven steps across the hardwood floor. I imagined Ethan's knees trembling as badly as mine were, wondered how he managed to walk at all. His arms were probably around Kieran, as desperate to touch him as he was for someone to hold him up.

They moved slowly down the hall, sharp hisses of breath punctuating the rustle of clothing and shuffle of feet. When they paused not far from my door, I wasn't worried that they'd hear me breathing, since I wasn't breathing at all, but my heart pounded so hard I was sure they'd hear that. Even if they did, though, I didn't imagine they'd notice, not if Ethan was kissing him the way I was sure he was. I could almost taste Ethan's semen on Kieran's tongue, and the very thought made my mouth water.

They continued down the hall until the sharp click of Kieran's bedroom door returned the house to silence. I finally managed to stand on my own two feet and got ready for bed. Unlike the ceiling that divided my bedroom from Ethan's, the walls and bathroom between Kieran's and mine were enough to drown out all but the most desperate groans. For that, I was thankful; I wasn't sure how much more I could take tonight.

As I lay in the mostly silent darkness and relived that strange, hot experience, an uncomfortable knot settled in my stomach.

I wanted to tell myself that it was Kieran who had turned me on. It was the sight of him sucking Ethan's cock like there was nothing in the world he'd rather do, devouring him with the same enthusiasm as every time he went down on me. It was the anticipation of having him again. It was simple voyeurism.

But no matter how much I rationalized it to myself, deep down I couldn't help but wonder:

If it was Kieran who had turned me on, then why had I spent the entire time thinking of Ethan?

Chapter Sixteen

The next evening, Kieran was already gone for the night when Ethan came home from work.

We neither spoke nor looked at each other as we went about making ourselves something to eat. Our kitchen was so big it practically needed its own area code, but tonight, it seemed much too small. I stood in front of the drawer that held something he needed. We both went for the cutting board at the same time. It didn't matter how big the room was, we couldn't stay out of each other's way.

Mercifully, we finally managed to get everything we needed and retreated to opposite ends of the counter to make our respective dinners. Then he took his and headed out of the kitchen, taking the awkward silence with him. He was almost gone, almost out of the room, and I could just about release my breath, but then he stopped.

Pausing in the doorway, he rocked back and forth from his heels to the balls of his feet as if he couldn't quite decide whether his next step would be forward or back. After a moment, he settled on the latter. He set down his plate and folded his arms, resting his hip against the counter.

"Look, I'm, um." He paused, clearing his throat and looking at the floor before finally offering me a cautious glance. "Sorry about last night."

I shrugged. "It was probably bound to happen."

He laughed half-heartedly. "Yeah, maybe so. But, still, if I'd known you were going to be home..."

"Don't worry about it." I shifted my weight. "Really, it wasn't a big deal."

Resting his hands on the counter beside his hips, he relaxed a little and even chanced a smirk. "You didn't seem to mind the view."

I laughed and dropped my gaze, certain my cheeks were bright red. "I guess I can't complain." I silently prayed he'd let the conversation end and continue his path out of the kitchen, but he didn't move.

"So apparently," he said, "we're sharing our house and our housemate."

My eyes flicked up, meeting his. "Yeah, I guess we are." I let out a sharp breath of laughter. "Well, if he can handle both of us..."

Ethan chuckled. "Can't imagine it's that difficult for someone like him to keep up with two old men."

I rolled my eyes. "Come on, we're not *that* old." I paused. "Well, okay, *I'm* not that—"

"Hey, fuck you." He laughed. "I've only got two years on you."

I shrugged. "At least I'm not over forty."

He gave me a playful glare. "Keep it up, and you won't live to *see* forty."

We both laughed, then fell silent, but it wasn't that awkward, uncomfortable silence to which I'd grown accustomed. I couldn't remember the last time we'd had a conversation like this, exchanging good-natured swipes and almost being relaxed around each other.

"Well, I can't blame you for going after him," I said. "I would have."

He laughed. "You did, from the sound of it."

I shook my head. "He came after me."

Ethan blinked. "Damn, I had to work for it."

"Oh please. By the looks of it, you had him wrapped around your finger that first night."

With a knowing smirk, he said, "Yeah, but he still took a bit of work. Guess I'm out of practice." Our eyes met, and his quickly darted away. Clearing his throat, he shifted the subject safely away from *us* and to the marginally more comfortable topic of *him*. "Christ, that man is incredible with his mouth." His cheeks colored, and I guessed the subject change was a little less awkward in his mind than when he said it.

But I followed suit. At least we had something in common for once. I shook my head and whistled. "Yeah he is."

He grinned but avoided my eyes. "All he needs to make it even better is a—"

I let my tongue stud rattle loudly against my teeth and grinned to myself when he shivered.

"You read my mind." He still didn't look at me.

"I know your tastes." My humor suddenly faded as I realize we'd stepped right back into the uncomfortable territory of our past sex life. Our past *life*. I stared at the tiles beneath my feet.

"Yeah," he said flatly. "I guess you do."

What a surreal feeling, being this uncomfortable talking about something that used to be as natural for us as breathing. Then again, we'd never compared notes on a mutual lover before, because it had just been us. *Good God, could this whole living arrangement get* any *weirder?*

"Anyway," he said. "Sorry we, um, weren't a bit more

discreet last night."

"It's okay."

"Though I have to admit," he said with a sly grin, "it was kind of hot having someone watching, even if it was just for a minute."

I laughed and rolled my eyes. "I never thought you were the exhibitionist type."

"I'm not. But I think it was a little different last night."

I swallowed. "How so?"

He shrugged. "I guess I thought it would be more awkward than it was, but it wasn't, because it was you."

"What?" I laughed, hoping it would cue him to do the same, but he kept a straight face. Clearing my throat, I said, "What do you mean?"

"I mean, it would have embarrassed the hell out of me had it been anyone else." He shifted his weight. "But since it was you..."

Blood pounded in my ears and I gripped the edge of the counter. "Ethan—"

"In fact," he said, pushing himself away from the counter with his hip, "it got me thinking."

"Thinking about what?" I asked, eyeing him.

"Just..." He paused, shrugging again, this time with one shoulder. His lip curled into that smirk, that smirk that turned my knees to water. "...thinking."

I swallowed hard as he started toward me.

"I hadn't realized how long it's been." He trailed his fingers along the edge of the counter as he came closer. His eyes never left mine, and every step he took was slow. Deliberate. A crossing of lines long since drawn. "Months, hasn't it?"

I drew back slightly, and the cabinets stopped me. "Yeah. Something like that." Holding onto the counter for balance, I watched his fingers drifting closer, casually shortening the strip of granite that divided his hand from mine. My heart pounded when he stopped just inches away from me, and I sucked in a breath as his hand drifted over mine and also stopped.

"Ethan, we—"

My breath caught when his thumb ran along the side of my hand.

"I know. We can't." His hand was on the move again, sliding over the back of mine. "We shouldn't." Across my wrist. "But I have to admit..." Up my arm. "...I can't help but wonder..."

I closed my eyes as his hand followed the curve of my neck into my hair. Even with my eyes closed, I sensed him coming closer, knew he was coming closer...

"It's been a long, long time," he whispered, his breath warming the side of my throat and his voice thrumming against my skin. "Entirely too long." His lips touched my neck, planting a single, tender kiss just above my collarbone.

"Jesus, Ethan..." I tried to keep my grip on the counter when he kissed my neck again, but against my will, my arms went around him. I'd almost forgotten how much I loved his lips against my skin or the coolness of his breath rushing past when he breathed me in. I didn't want this to turn me on, but it did.

"I know what you were thinking last night," he whispered, trailing kisses up the side of my neck to the underside of my jaw. "I saw it in your eyes."

I bit my lip, sucking in a breath when he flicked his tongue across my earlobe. "What was I thinking?"

"Seeing us like that, it turned you on, didn't it?" He pressed his hips against mine, and I shivered. He was as hard as I was *and holy hell I want him.*

"Of course it did." I struggled to keep my teeth from chattering.

He raised his head and looked at me, his face just inches from mine. "You wanted him to suck your cock like that, didn't you?"

I moistened my lips and looked him in the eye. "Not quite."

His eyebrows jumped. "Oh?"

"I didn't want to take your place." I put my hands on his face and leaned closer to him. "I wanted to take *his.*"

And for the first time in ages, I kissed Ethan.

Chapter Seventeen

We were still for a moment.

Then he parted my lips with the tip of his tongue, and our bodies melted back into slow, fluid motion, our hands sliding across skin and fabric as we pulled each other closer. Our glacial slowness contradicted the intense need that pulsed just beneath the surface, but I wasn't sure we could handle moving any faster. As it was, his deepening kiss bombarded my senses with forgotten familiarity. The coarseness of his jaw against mine, the faint, lingering hints of the heady aftershave he always wore, the way his fingertips brushed across my five o'clock shadow.

When he broke the kiss, his hands rested on either side of my neck, keeping me close and gently forcing me to hold his gaze even when it became too intense. For a moment, he stared at me with something akin to disbelief. His shoulders rose and fell slightly with his deep, rapid breaths.

Between us, the air crackled with dozens of unasked questions, all of which boiled down to one: Should we?

For all our inability to communicate, there were times when I swore we could read each other's thoughts. Looking into his eyes now, with his kiss lingering on my tongue, I knew this was one of those times.

It didn't matter if we should. We were.

"I know we ended things." His lips brushed mine. "I know we probably shouldn't do this..." His fingers trembled against my neck. "But, I can't help it. I want you." As soon as he kissed me again, there was nothing left to discuss. He wanted it, I wanted it, that was all that mattered.

I pushed his shoulders, he pulled my shirt, and we clumsily started out of the kitchen toward the hall. With my body weight, I shoved him up against the doorframe, and he grunted as his back made contact with it. I pushed his shirt over his head and kissed his neck and shoulders and *sweet mother of God, I forgot how much I love these shoulders.*

He pushed himself off the doorframe and guided us both into the hall. Kissing and touching, kicking shoes and pulling off shirts, fumbling with belts and stumbling over feet. It didn't matter where anything landed or what we bumped into on the way; the only thing that mattered was getting out of these clothes and into a bed.

He passed my bedroom door, no doubt intending to go upstairs to the room we once shared, but I grabbed his arm, then his shoulders, pulling him to me, into a kiss, into the bedroom. There, he pushed me up against the door, using our combined body weight to close it. The door was cold against my back, but it was the heat of his body and his breath that made me shiver.

I tried to guide him toward the bed, to get us across the narrow space that divided us from where we needed to be, but he didn't move. "Bed," I said, panting against his lips.

"Right here," he growled. "I can't wait, I—" He paused and looked around. "Shit, you have condoms in here, I hope?"

Wetting my lips, I nodded toward the nightstand, which was a foot or so away from us.

"Thank God." He leaned to the side and opened the drawer.

As he rifled around in it, he said, "Stay there. Stay right there."

I couldn't have gone anywhere anyway. My need for him occupied every bit of my focus, and just like last night, the door against my back was the only thing keeping me standing.

Tearing foil made my mouth water.

"Wait," I said.

He stopped, condom in hand, eyebrows lifted.

"Come here," I whispered, reaching for his arm. I wrapped my other hand around his cock.

"Oh fuck, Rhett." He moaned, closing his eyes. "Fuck, that's—oh God, I want to fuck you."

"I know." Before he could object any further, I went to my knees.

"Rhett, please, I—*oh God...*"

I ran my tongue stud along the underside of his cock, from base to tip, and his protests turned into breathless moans. Stroking with one hand, I licked and sucked his cock, finding all the places and doing all the things I knew he loved: Fluttering my tongue just beneath the head. Rolling the piercing up and down the shaft. *Almost* deep-throating him.

The salt of his skin and the rhythm of his pulse against my tongue made my head spin. Every helpless moan just turned me on that much more. I couldn't get enough of him.

"Wait," he said. "Rhett, stand up, stand up, please..."

I didn't want to stop, but the need in his voice was even more arousing than the taste of his cock, so I did as he asked. As soon as I was on my feet, he slammed me up against the door again and kissed me, crushing my lips with his and drawing my tongue into his mouth.

Just as abruptly as he'd started, he pulled back, cursing as he tried to get the condom on with trembling hands. He managed, though, and reached for the lube bottle.

"Turn around," he said through his teeth. "I'm not waiting another fucking minute."

I turned around and put my hands on the door, biting my lip as the lube bottle clicked shut, then rattled and fell off the edge of the nightstand. Neither of us bothered to reach for it.

Ethan put his hands on my hips and nudged my legs apart with his knee. Cool lube touched my skin, and I couldn't even breathe, knowing he was about to fuck me. *My God, it's been too damned long, way too long, fuck, I need this...*

"Oh Jesus," he breathed, pushing into me slowly. "Oh fucking hell..." He took a few gentle, easy strokes, then gained speed, groaning as he fucked me. Hard. *Harder.*

My fingers tried to claw at the door, seeking something— anything—to hold onto. "Fuck, Ethan, that's incredible." I moaned. "Don't stop, don't..."

"I won't, I won't, not until...oh God, I want...Jesus, Rhett, you feel so fucking good." He buried his face against my neck, every vibration of his voice and brush of his coarsely stubbled jaw reminding me in no uncertain terms that this was *Ethan.* Ethan was the one whispering deliciously filthy things into my ear, Ethan was the one slamming his cock deep inside me, Ethan was the one who was about to make me come as only Ethan could.

I shuddered. "Fuck, I'm—"

"Don't you dare come yet," he growled. "We're not done, don't you fucking *dare.*"

I tried to breathe in, but he thrust into me so hard he knocked the air right out of my lungs. Gasping for breath, I said, "Fuck, you're not..." Another gasp. "You're not giving me much choice."

"Not yet." He was pleading now. "I haven't felt..." He groaned, a tremor interrupting his rhythm for a split second. "...haven't felt your cock in too damned long..." His fingers gripped my hips even tighter, and he released a sharp breath against my neck. "I want...I need..." He moaned, and his cock pulsed inside me. "*Fuck me.*"

That alone, the sheer desperation in his voice, nearly made me come. He had always worn desperation well; there was nothing sexier than Ethan pleading for more, more, please, God, *more*. A heartbeat before I would have lost it, though, he groaned and came, taking one final thrust when one *more* would have driven me over the edge.

Still trembling and panting against my shoulder, he begged, "Fuck me. Please, Rhett, fuck me..."

All I could do was nod, and he exhaled as he pulled out slowly. He got rid of the condom as I fished another from the drawer and tore the wrapper. As I rolled it on, he picked up the fallen lube bottle, handed it to me and gave me an inquisitive look.

"Bend over the bed," I said, pouring some lube into my hand. While I put on lube, he did as I said, turning and putting his hands on the bed. Just the thought of fucking him, of being inside him after all this time, was almost enough to put me over the edge, but I took a deep breath and kept myself in control.

Standing behind him, I put a hand on his lower back and guided my cock to him. He shivered when we made contact, released a breath when I slid into him.

It didn't matter that I'd been with Kieran a few times recently. The first long, slow stroke I took inside Ethan may as well have been the first in months. I'd forgotten just how good he felt, just how incredible he looked. As I withdrew and pushed in again, I had to close my eyes just to keep from coming quite yet. Watching my cock sliding in and out of him was just too damned much. *Jesus, I'd forgotten how hot you are, Ethan.*

"Oh God, oh God..." My voice shook, and it wasn't just from my rapid thrusts. Every time he moaned, every time I drove my cock deep inside him, something in me fell apart a little more and I lost my sanity piece by shattering piece.

He rocked back against me, moving his hips in time with mine, and all I could do was hold on for dear life, surrender, and, with one last thrust and a helpless moan, come inside him.

For a moment, I couldn't move. Breathing was almost too much, but I managed. Slowly, the electricity surging through my nerves eased and my orgasm subsided.

My mind was a mess of disarray and disbelief, but as the pieces fell back into place, as Ethan and I separated and my body once again remembered how to move, awareness crept in. Awareness, but not understanding.

I knew what had happened.

I didn't know why, or if it should have, or what would happen next.

All I knew was that I had just fucked my ex-boyfriend and *loved* it.

Chapter Eighteen

Afterward, we lay in silence. The adrenaline had worn off, I'd caught my breath, but still my pulse raced. Whether or not we should have, we had. Now what?

Someone had to break the ice sooner or later. It might as well have been me, so I turned my head toward him. "Well, this wasn't what I was expecting."

He laughed. "No kidding."

"So." I cleared my throat. "Where do we go from here?"

The laughter faded into a sigh. "I don't know." He rubbed his eyes with his thumb and forefinger, then folded his hands across his chest and looked at me. "I really don't know."

"Do you think this is a good idea?"

"What? This time?" he said. "Or doing it again?"

"I, um, well, either, I guess."

"Not much we can do about this time." He shrugged. "The question is, do we keep doing it?"

"Do we?"

"Well, why not?" He turned on his side and propped himself up on one arm. "Look, we're stuck living together. We're sharing a house. We're sharing a man, for God's sake." Another shrug, this time with a hint of a grin on his lips. "So, who says we can't fuck once in a while?"

I laughed half-heartedly. "Is it really that simple?"

"It's only as complicated as we make it, Rhett."

"And we seem to have quite a knack for making the simple into something complicated."

"Okay, I'll give you that." His expression shifted a little closer to serious. "But if you think about it, it's simpler than anything else about all of this. I mean, let's face it, fighting or not, when we actually do it, sex is the one thing we've always gotten right." He raised his eyebrows. "So why not enjoy it?"

Something in the back of my mind tried to protest, but I couldn't argue with Ethan's simple, straightforward logic. This was, after all, the least tense we'd been in recent memory. No sniping, no icy glares. There was still an undeniable distance between us, a line drawn when we ended our relationship, but for once it felt more like a boundary and less like a battle line. A sexual relationship wasn't the same as what we had before, but it beat the hell out of a rivalry.

"Yeah, I think I can live with this." I smiled. "So what about Kieran? Do we work out a custody schedule?"

Ethan laughed. "I guess we'll just play that by ear."

"Could be interesting if we both decide we want him on the same night." I chuckled.

Ethan's eyes lost focus for a second, and the lines in his forehead hinted at deep concentration. Before I could ask what he was thinking, though, his lips curled into a smirk that sent a pleasant shudder down my spine. Sliding a hand around my waist, he leaned toward me and said against my lips, "That could *definitely* get interesting..."

Chapter Nineteen

A few nights later, Kieran and I both had the evening off.

"You two have quite a collection of DVDs," he said over his shoulder as he admired the well-stocked tower.

"They're mostly Ethan's." I kicked back on the couch with a glass of wine. "He's a bit of a film connoisseur."

"So I see. Certainly an odd mix. I can't say I've ever seen *Quills*, *Resident Evil* and *The Phantom of the Opera* on the same shelf."

I laughed. "Well, we both have rather eclectic taste."

Over his shoulder, he gave me a knowing look, then turned back to the DVDs. "I was in the mood to watch something. How about you?"

I am watching something. My cheeks burned at the thought, and I quickly cleared my throat. "Yeah, sure. Anything in particular?"

He shrugged. "You've probably seen every one of these a dozen times or so."

"Not really. Maybe half."

He pulled one case off the rack and flipped it over. "*Walk the Line*, huh? I haven't seen this one all the way through."

I blinked. "You haven't seen *Walk the Line*?"

He offered a sheepish look. "I've tried a few times, but I

kept getting distracted. My ex had a thing for Joaquin Phoenix and, for some reason, we never could make it through this film."

Putting up my hands, I said, "I'll do the best I can not to distract you."

"Well, if you do," he said, popping the DVD case open, "that's why the good Lord gave us the pause button." He knelt to put the disc in the player.

I drained my glass, set it on the coffee table and picked up the remote. He hit the lights, then sat beside me as I started the movie.

We sat close together on the couch, and I put my arm around his shoulders. As soon his body warmed mine, making me hyperaware of every place we made contact, I forgot what DVD we were watching. *Something tells me we'll be needing that pause button.*

Kieran didn't even wait for the starting credits to end. He reached across his own lap and rested his hand on my thigh, moving his thumb back and forth along the outer seam of my jeans. Every fragment of my awareness was concentrated on that gentle motion, the vague hint of heat through denim, the parody of skin-to-skin contact. My eyes wouldn't even focus on the screen.

He lifted his head off my shoulder and raised his chin to look at me. When I looked down, thinking he was about to speak, he kissed me.

His kiss wasn't aggressive at all. In fact, it was almost passive, his lips moving with mine, but waiting for me to make the next move. I cupped his jaw, and my tongue gently urged his lips apart. As my fingers moved to the back of his neck and into his hair, he put his arm around me. His other hand slid over my leg and drifted up the inside of my thigh, stopping just shy of my cock. Even as the kiss deepened, he kept his hand where it was. Close, but not touching. There, but not. Teasing by proximity.

Pulling him to me, I turned my entire body to face him and, in doing so, pushed my cock against his hand. I gasped, shivering as we unexpectedly made the contact I'd craved. His fingers tightened and released gently, just enough movement to say *I'm touching you and I want you to feel me touching you.*

Then, as suddenly as we'd touched, both his hand and mouth pulled away. I wanted to grab his shirt and bring him back to me, but then he licked his lips and gave me that sexy, sexy grin. I couldn't even protest when he sat up and leaned toward the coffee table.

"Thank God for the pause button." He picked up the remote and clicked off whatever movie it was we weren't watching. When he came back to me, his kiss was different. His mouth was no longer passive, and he no longer waited for me to make a move. Instead, his lips and tongue assumed command. A moment later, his body followed suit when he shifted his weight, gently nudging me against the back of the couch. One hand drifted down my side, then followed my belt to the buckle, and I took in a sharp breath through my nose as he made quick work of both buckle and zipper.

He stroked my cock gently for a moment, still kissing me, and I didn't have to ask what he had in mind when he sat up and moved to the floor.

My voice shook as I said, "You love sucking cock, don't you?"

"There's nothing in the world I like better." Before I could respond, his mouth was around my cock.

I moaned. He completely engulfed my senses, summoning my full attention to every place his hands and mouth made contact with my skin. He read my every response perfectly, knowing exactly when to give and when to take, when to bring me to the edge and when to bring me back. All I could do was lose myself in everything he did.

A low, familiar rumble vibrated up through the floor, barely registering at the edges of my awareness. When the sound cut off, the nearly inaudible purr of an engine remained for a second before it too was silenced. Then the garage door opener rumbled to life again.

I couldn't decide if Ethan's arrival made me want to laugh or panic, but Kieran's mouth on my cock precluded either of those things from happening. Something in my mind tried to ask if Ethan was home unexpectedly, if I should have known, if *oh God, Kieran, do that again...*

A door opened and closed downstairs. A momentary break in his rhythm told me Kieran was aware that we were no longer alone in the house, but he didn't stop. In fact, he doubled his efforts, squeezing harder with his lips and circling faster with his tongue as if to distract me from Ethan.

And he very nearly succeeded. I closed my eyes and let my head fall back, letting Kieran carry my sanity away. The man's mouth was second to none, and when I was at the mercy of his lips and tongue, it was almost impossible to think.

Almost. In spite of my distraction, Ethan's presence was palpable, a thrum of *something* in space that had been, moments ago, empty.

When that presence moved into the living room, I didn't have to look. I knew. The few scattered shards of my awareness that weren't focused on Kieran's mouth instantly honed in on Ethan. He'd stopped, this much I knew. Maybe amusement had narrowed his eyes and drawn the corners of his mouth into a smirk. Maybe his lips were parted and his eyes wide with disbelief. Whatever his expression, he was there. Still and silent, but *there.*

When he moved again, he didn't continue down the hall as I had done when I'd walked in on them the other night. Instead, he made a wide arc across the floor, passing behind Kieran and around the back of the couch. He was close by. Getting closer. Closer still. The near-silent rustle of shifting fabric disappeared in the pounding of my heart.

Even though I knew he was there, *right there*, I wasn't prepared when his hands slid over my shoulders and sent shivers down my spine. Shivers that rippled down to my cock, and everything Kieran did sent those shivers right back up just as Ethan's lips touched my neck. I gasped and only the hands on my shoulders kept me from levitating off the couch.

I reached up and slid my hand around the back of Ethan's neck and when I turned my head, he kissed me. Full-on, no hesitation, devouring my mouth the way Kieran devoured my cock.

Kieran looked up, but his hands didn't stop. I broke my kiss with Ethan and looked down, unsure what to expect in Kieran's expression. When our eyes met, though, his were full of hunger and lust. If he was nervous or even surprised, he didn't show it. He moistened his lips, then went down on me again, sucking my cock with even more desperate enthusiasm than before.

I reached back and pulled at Ethan's shirt. He leaned forward so I could pull it over his head, and after I threw it aside, he slid his hands down my chest and pulled my shirt free. As soon as my shirt was gone, his mouth was over mine again.

Ethan's tongue teased my piercing as Kieran's teased the head of my cock. Every time one of them exhaled, it warmed my skin, and every time one of them moaned or growled, it echoed through my nerve endings. With one hand on the back of Ethan's neck and one in Kieran's hair, holding on to both for dear life while I tasted one and both tasted me, I had never been so aroused. No one gave head like Kieran, no one kissed like Ethan, and if I had died in that moment, I would have gone a happy man.

The pure, liquid lightning coursing up and down my spine brought a string of whispered profanity right to the tip of my tongue, but Ethan's mouth silenced it. I was sure, at any moment, that I was going to come, but Kieran expertly held me back, promising with every stroke of his tongue that he wasn't done with me yet.

"Oh God," I breathed against Ethan's lips. I held the back of his neck tighter, and he dipped his head to kiss behind my ear. His hand drifted down my chest and his fingertip made light circles around my nipple.

"This is the sexiest thing I've ever seen," he murmured. "Watching you, knowing exactly what he's doing because he's done it to me..." He kissed the base of my neck. "Kieran, I'd fucking beg you to suck my cock like that right here and now, but watching you do it to him is just too damned hot."

Kieran responded with a low moan that vibrated across my skin before he deep-throated me.

Ethan wasn't finished. "I want you both so fucking bad right now..." He nipped the side of my neck, "...just watching the two of you, I'm so damned turned on..." He exhaled hard, warming my skin and making me shiver. With every word, his voice descended to a deeper growl. "...I want to taste you both, I want to fuck you both, I want you both to fuck me."

The more Ethan said, the more Kieran stroked and sucked my cock.

"Don't stop," I moaned. "Jesus Christ, don't stop."

"No one's stopping," Ethan growled, his stubble brushing the side of my jaw. "He's going to make you come, and I'm..." He sucked in a breath, pausing to kiss me before continuing in a trembling voice, "...if he's not careful, he's going to make me come too."

Kieran shivered, and a ragged rush of cool breath whooshed across my skin as he moved even faster. He was past the point of give and take, of holding back to draw it out, and there was no resisting even if I wanted to, especially with Ethan's kiss on top of it all. My heart pounded, my body shook with unreleased tension, and every nerve in my body turned to pure electricity.

"Come, Rhett," Ethan said, the words vibrating against my lips. His voice was somewhere between an aroused whisper and a desperate plea. "Let me see what he does to you."

Ethan kissed me.

Kieran ran his tongue around the head of my cock.

I *lost it.*

My cock pulsed against Kieran's lips and my voice drowned in Ethan's mouth as my sanity buckled. My eyes rolled back and my spine melted and everything seemed to explode and collapse at once.

With one final shudder, I sank against the back of the couch and released a long breath. Ethan released my shoulders and stood as Kieran joined me on the couch.

"Oh my God," I whispered, licking my lips to get one last taste of Ethan's kiss. As Ethan moved around the couch, Kieran sat beside me and kissed me. My head still spun, and I struggled to catch my breath, but kissing was more important than breathing, so I tangled my fingers in his hair and let the tip of his tongue draw mine into his mouth.

The taste of my own semen on his tongue made this all real. It wasn't just a fantasy, this had really happened. And, as Ethan kissed between my shoulder blades, working his way up to my neck, it was *still* happening.

I pushed up Kieran's shirt and broke the kiss to pull it over his head. When I reached back to drop his shirt over the back of the couch, Ethan leaned over me, cupped the back of Kieran's neck and pulled him into a kiss. So much for catching my breath after that incredible orgasm, because as I stared at them, all the air went out of my lungs anyway.

Watching two men kiss was always something that turned me on, but this went beyond that. Far beyond that. I knew how they both kissed. I knew exactly what it felt like when Ethan ran the tip of his tongue across Kieran's lower lip, and when Kieran's cheeks hollowed, I shivered because I knew his tongue was slipping into Ethan's mouth.

I sat up and kissed Kieran's neck. He gasped, and Ethan seized the opportunity to kiss me. Kieran immediately went for my neck, sending shivers down my spine with every touch of his lips. When I turned to kiss Kieran, Ethan ran the tip of his tongue along my collarbone. When they in turn kissed again, I found that sensitive spot behind Ethan's ear and flicked my tongue across it.

The next time Ethan's lips met mine, Kieran pulled back and stood, but he didn't go far. He sat on the other side of Ethan and, a second later, Ethan gasped, throwing his head back as his spine straightened suddenly. I craned my neck to see what had startled him.

Kieran's lips and fingertips worked their way up Ethan's back. Ethan bit his lip and closed his eyes, whimpering softly as Kieran's lips paused just below his hair.

"Lean back," Kieran whispered in his ear. I don't know if

Ethan consciously obeyed or if it was a passive response, his body completely surrendered and at the mercy of Kieran's whims, but obey he did. I followed, kissing Ethan deeply while Kieran moved again.

Without even looking, I knew exactly what Kieran was doing. Ethan's belt buckle jingled. Then his separating zipper made his breath and mine catch. He held my face in both hands, digging his fingers into the back of my neck. *Don't you dare pull away*, he seemed to say. *I need you so I remember how to breathe.*

When Ethan's entire body seized and he pulled the breath out of my lungs, I knew Kieran's mouth was working its incredible magic. Ethan's fingers twitched in my hair and our lips occasionally separated when he released a sudden, sharp breath. He held me tighter as his deep, delirious moans reverberated against my mouth.

His head fell against the back of the couch and his eyes shut tight. As much as I wanted to kiss him again, his face mesmerized me. His lips alternated between tightening into a grimace and parting with the release of breath. Once or twice, he looked up, his eyes seeming to lose focus. Then twin lines appeared between his eyebrows just before his eyes closed again.

"Oh God," he breathed. A shudder worked its way through him, and his eyes screwed shut as his back then neck arched. I bent and kissed his exposed throat, tasting every tremor and moan beneath the sheen of perspiration on my way up the side of his neck. I stopped just shy of that spot behind his ear, keeping my lips against his skin but not touching him there, not yet.

"It's my turn, Ethan." My lips barely touched his skin as I spoke. "Let me see what he does to you."

"Oh my God," he moaned, sounding on the verge of madness or tears. "Oh my God..."

"Show me," I whispered, trailing my fingertips across his chest as my lips inched closer to that sweet spot behind his ear. "Show me you like it as much as I do."

"Oh...fuck..." he moaned. He whimpered softly, then shuddered, and when he gasped, I knew he was right there, right on the edge, and that's when I ran the tip of my tongue around the spot behind his ear. In that instant, he came so violently his body nearly flew up off the couch, but my arm across his chest kept him still, kept him here.

A long sigh signaled his return to terra firma, and his body relaxed.

As soon as Kieran rejoined us on the couch, Ethan sat up and kissed him, holding onto him with trembling hands and gasping for breath between kisses.

"I have never met anyone who likes giving head as much as you do," he slurred, releasing Kieran and sinking back to the couch.

Kieran grinned. "Like I told Rhett, it's my favorite thing in the world."

"Well, rest assured," Ethan said, closing his eyes for a moment. "No good deed goes unpunished." Then he looked at me and grinned. No, *smirked*. That filthy, sexy smirk. "I've got the king-sized bed. Assuming we can all still manage to get up the stairs..." He trailed off, but the lift of his eyebrows and the extra twist of his smirk finished the question.

Neither Kieran nor I had to answer.

Chapter Twenty

As soon as we were in Ethan's bedroom, he and I descended on Kieran. Ethan stood behind him and kissed his neck and shoulders. I stood in front and tangled my fingers in Kieran's hair as I kissed his mouth.

Ethan reached around with one hand and unbuckled Kieran's belt while I took care of the zipper. I just barely touched his cock, trailing my fingertips up and down, up and down. Then I grasped it gently and stroked a couple times, just enough to make him gasp, before resuming my featherlight touches.

"Fucking tease," he growled.

"Tease?" I said with a cough of laughter. "Did you hear that, Ethan?"

"Yes, I did." He nipped Kieran's shoulder hard enough to make him take in a hiss of breath. "Maybe you should show him how much of a tease you can be."

"Maybe I should." I continued with my barely there touches, kissing one side of Kieran's neck while Ethan kissed the other. Kieran moaned softly as I closed my hand around his cock, but I still kept my strokes gentle and uneven. His hips tried to follow my hand, tried to match a rhythm that didn't exist. Chewing his lip, he released another moan that was probably as much from frustration as arousal, and I grinned against his neck.

"Maybe I should stop teasing him," I whispered. "What do you think?"

Ethan laughed and instantly created goose bumps on Kieran's skin. "I think he deserves to have his cock sucked, don't you?"

"After everything he's done," I said, "I think you're right." Kieran's cock twitched in my hand, and his breath caught. I dropped to my knees, steadying him with one hand on his hip as I circled the head of his cock with my tongue.

"Oh fuck," he moaned. The tip of my tongue explored every ridge and contour of his cock as if it was uncharted territory, as if I'd never tasted him before. My piercing traced the same path, rolling smoothly over those same ridges and contours. When I circled the head of his cock, I alternated. Once around with my tongue, once with the piercing, over and over until his knees shook.

I glanced up. Kieran's head was turned and he kissed Ethan over his shoulder, his free hand grasping the back of Ethan's neck as mine had done earlier. Their lips separated for a half second, just long enough to let me see Ethan's tongue slide into Kieran's mouth. I couldn't help but moan against Kieran's cock, making him shudder. Or maybe it was Ethan's kiss that did it.

Then Ethan murmured something to Kieran, speaking so quietly in his ear that I sensed the presence of his voice, but couldn't make out the words. Kieran's responses told me all I needed to know, though. His breathing became less steady, his hand trembled in my hair, the telltale saltiness met my tongue. It was impossible to tell whether Ethan's mouth or mine triggered which responses, but I didn't care. Kieran was unraveling, and that was all that mattered.

His body jerked as if he'd been shocked, then again. His cock pulsed in my mouth, so I gave him everything I had.

Ethan spoke again, the words just beyond my reach, his voice creating a low, growling undercurrent beneath the tension building in every breath Kieran tried to draw. Kieran's knees shook and his hips mirrored my forward and back motions and his cock twitched and, just as he released a helpless, breathless whimper, salty-sweet semen shot across my tongue.

I kept going, stroking and sucking, making sure his orgasm lasted as long as humanly possible and only stopping when he finally begged me to.

While he caught his breath, I stood. Before I was even fully on my feet, Ethan grabbed me and kissed me deeply, desperately, grasping my hair and the back of my neck as his tongue sought every last taste of Kieran.

Fingers wrapped around my cock, and I gasped. A second later, so did Ethan. We both looked down. Kieran stroked both of us, then ran his tongue around the head of Ethan's cock, sending a shiver through him before he did the same to me.

"Fuck," Ethan whispered. Our eyes met, and a low growl emerged from the back of his throat as he tightened his grasp on my hair and kissed me. For the second time that night, I was lost in the overwhelming twin sensations of Kieran's mouth on my cock and Ethan's lips against mine.

This time, though, Ethan was just as helplessly aroused, responding to both my mouth and Kieran's. Whenever Kieran's mouth left my cock, Ethan gasped. Then he'd relax slightly and it would be my turn to tremble as Kieran's tongue swirled around the head of my cock.

Much more of that and I was going to come again, but I wasn't ready for that yet.

Looking Ethan in the eye, I said, "I want to fuck you."

"Please do," he said in a hoarse whisper. He held my gaze a moment longer, then closed his eyes and let out a breath as Kieran's mouth moved from my cock to his. I stepped back, and they both released me. The sudden break in contact was jarring, nearly enough to make me stumble on my way to the drawer that held the condoms. My hands shook as I tore the wrapper, so desperate was I to be inside Ethan, to be touching either of them again.

As I rolled the condom on, Kieran continued sucking Ethan's cock. I was tempted to suggest that Ethan move, that he get on his hands and knees so I could fuck him good and hard the way I knew he wanted, but the low moan that escaped his parted lips gave me a better idea.

After I'd put on some lube, making sure to leave the bottle on the bed within reach in case I needed more, I stood behind Ethan and put my hands on his hips. When I gently nudged his legs apart with my knee, his spine straightened. He glanced over his shoulder, eyes wide with surprise.

"I want you just like this," I said.

He started to speak, but when I pressed my cock against him, he simply moaned and put a hand on the bedpost to steady himself.

"Oh Jesus," he breathed as I pushed into him slowly.

"Oh, fuck, you feel good." I closed my eyes and tried to stay in the present, but my head spun faster with every inch I gained and I went further out of my mind every time I withdrew and pushed back in. I took long, smooth strokes at first, just trying to keep myself from coming or collapsing under the weight of how fucking incredible this was.

Ethan's knees trembled, nearly buckling. Mine weren't much steadier and, for a moment, I thought they were about to give out, that he and I were both on the verge of going down. I could keep my own balance, but I wasn't sure about both of us. Then Kieran stood, grasping Ethan's shoulders and kissing him, using his body to keep Ethan—and me—upright. Ethan gripped Kieran's shoulders for balance and returned his kiss.

With this new stability, I was free to focus less on standing and more on fucking Ethan. Gritting my teeth and digging my fingers into his hips, I pounded him hard and fast, every moan and whimper nearly sending me out of my mind.

Kieran moaned as Ethan bent and kissed his neck. Ethan's hand disappeared between them, and Kieran gasped, throwing his head back as Ethan's shoulder rose and fell in time with my rapid thrusts.

I couldn't hold back, not when they were both so turned on, when they looked so damned hot, when Ethan felt so fucking good and his back arched that way and Kieran's lips parted with slurred profanities and my spine melted more with every stroke I took inside Ethan and—

"Oh fuck..." I groaned. I pulled Ethan's hips against mine, driving my cock as deep as I could, and came. His body still moved with the force of his own strokes on Kieran's cock, and that subtle motion, that vague hint of a perfect rhythm, drew out my orgasm until I thought I was going to pass out.

When I couldn't take anymore, I pulled out slowly, still gasping for breath.

As I got rid of the condom, Ethan kissed Kieran, holding the sides of his neck with trembling hands. "Now it's your turn." They exchanged grins and a brief kiss. Then Ethan turned to me. "Mind getting me a condom while you're there?"

I nodded and grabbed one out of the drawer, handing it to him as I walked past. He tore the wrapper with his teeth and quickly rolled the condom on. Then I tossed him the bottle of lube and leaned against the bed, pulling Kieran against me.

Holding his face in both hands, I kissed him deeply, passionately.

Just as earlier when I made out with Ethan while Kieran sucked him off, I could tell what Ethan was doing by the way Kieran responded. A shudder ran up, then down his spine, probably following Ethan's hands on his skin before they settled on Kieran's hips. The touch of cool lube was most likely what made him tense and gasp. Then he drew in a long, deep breath, and the low groan from Ethan told me he was slowly pushing his cock into Kieran.

As Ethan picked up speed, Kieran's body rocked against mine, echoing the rhythm and force of Ethan's deep, rapid thrusts. The harder Ethan fucked him, the more Kieran kissed me.

As he did, I looked over his shoulder. When I met Ethan's eyes, his lips parted and a shudder rippled through his body, then Kieran's, then mine. Never in my life had I seen such visible, insatiable arousal burning in someone's eyes as I did just then. I thought it turned me on to watch Kieran and Ethan kiss, but watching Ethan watch us was hot enough to take my breath away.

I kept one hand on Kieran's neck and reached between us with the other, stroking him just as Ethan had while I'd fucked him moments ago. Kieran moaned, throwing his head back. I kissed his neck and again looked right at Ethan. His brow knitted together and he wetted his lips. When I gently bit the base of Kieran's neck, Ethan bit his own lip.

My hand followed Ethan's rhythm exactly, speeding up when he did, slowing down when he did. Kieran's mouth sought mine and when our lips met, he kissed me so violently he probably would have made me come had I not already. The low moan that followed didn't register as a vibration against my lips, and when I opened my eyes, I realized it was Ethan's voice.

Jesus, you've never looked so fucking hot, Ethan. Exertion made the cords on his neck stand out, and his shoulders and biceps trembled. His mouth was somewhere between a grimace and an unspoken cry. Sweat rolled down his temples and the sides of his face. His eyebrows were pulled together and his eyes were wide. Wide and focused right on mine.

I shivered, and my rhythm faltered slightly, making Kieran's breath catch. I squeezed a little harder, stroked faster, and his cock twitched in my hand. Then, breaking the kiss with a throaty cry, he came, his body nearly collapsing against mine as his semen hit my wrist and forearm.

Ethan bit his lip and closed his eyes, obviously trying to stay in control just a little bit longer. He looked down, watching himself fuck Kieran, and released a breath, then another, his lips forming words I couldn't hear and he probably didn't even understand.

Then his eyes flicked up and met mine. I ran my tongue across the backs of my teeth, letting the stud rattle against them, and his eyes had only a split second to widen before they screwed shut and he slammed his cock deep into Kieran and roared.

Kieran collapsed against me, and Ethan slumped behind him, resting his forehead on Kieran's shoulder.

"Jesus fucking Christ," Ethan slurred. "That..." He exhaled, shuddering as he pulled out slowly.

"Was hot." Kieran raised his head and kissed me lightly while Ethan stepped away to get rid of the condom.

"I think 'hot' would be an understatement," I said. Kieran stood on wobbling knees and, with me gently guiding him, stumbled to the bed.

"Good thing we came all the way up here for the king-sized

bed." Kieran wiped sweat from his brow and almost fell onto the bed.

Still panting, Ethan laughed. "Okay, so we didn't quite make it to the bed." He collapsed onto it, one hand across his chest while he tried to catch his breath.

I sank onto the bed beside them. "Well, we got here eventually."

"Pity it wasn't until after," Ethan said.

"Just means when we get started again," Kieran said, "we'll have to make use of it. You know, to make the trip up the stairs worthwhile."

Ethan blinked. "When we get started again?"

Kieran grinned. "Don't tell me you old guys are tired already."

Ethan and I exchanged incredulous looks.

Ethan closed his eyes and brushed a drop of sweat off his temple. "Do me a favor, Kieran."

"What's that?" Kieran said.

Ethan grinned at me, then looked at Kieran. "Never, *ever* move out of this house."

Chapter Twenty-one

It was well after two in the morning before Kieran and I stumbled downstairs to our respective bedrooms. Exhausted and beyond satisfied, all I could think of was sleep. I collapsed into my bed and closed my eyes to answer the siren's call of sleep just as the last waning reserves of adrenaline wore off.

I'd barely closed my eyes when my rational mind got its second wind. Though my body was exhausted, my brain was suddenly wide awake.

Wide awake, and wondering what the hell had happened. *Did Ethan really walk in on Kieran and me and join in? Did we really just spend the last few hours in bed? Was that real?*

As reality set in, a strange feeling slowly unwound itself in my chest, a cold prelude to an epiphany I hadn't yet had. Every time my mind drifted back to the threesome—and it did, over and over again—my stomach turned. The unraveling chill became a heavy, sinking feeling, one I recognized as a physical manifestation of pure, icy regret.

I exhaled and closed my eyes, rubbing my forehead in a futile attempt to push away the thoughts that were quickly working their way to the front of my consciousness. *I just want to sleep. If I'm going to regret this, can't it wait?*

It couldn't, apparently.

Everything about tonight had been hot. There probably

didn't exist a more sexually compatible trio on the planet. Still, a million reasons why this shouldn't have happened ran through my mind. It was going to complicate things. Things were going to get weird between Ethan and me. And Kieran and me. And Ethan and Kieran. It was going be harder to live with them now, and even harder to watch them go.

I sighed and cursed under my breath.

Maybe this was all in my head. Maybe it was not unlike the paranoid worry that followed sexual experimentation in my youth. I was still settling into the reality of "I've done that", rather than the previous state of "I'd like to try that". A threesome was something new. Uncharted territory now charted. In the light of day, I'd realize it wasn't such a big deal. I'd enjoyed it, as had they, and it hadn't knocked the world off its axis.

With any luck, they were in agreement. None of this would feel weird in the light of day. We could go on without awkwardness. I'd realize I was worrying over nothing.

I hoped.

When I went into the kitchen a few hours later, though, my concerns were evidently valid.

Everything seemed louder than normal, echoing the way they would if I was hungover, though without the headache. Shuffling feet. Coffee pouring. The refrigerator door popping open, then closing with a dull thud. Everything was amplified because, aside from those minute sounds of the morning, the kitchen was silent.

No one spoke. No one looked at each other. Or rather, no one looked directly at each other. I caught Kieran casting a quick, surreptitious glance at Ethan. When my eyes darted toward Ethan, I dropped my gaze before he noticed. Kieran and I accidentally met eyes, but only for the split second it took to realize we had done so.

Above the quiet cacophony of morning routines, the air was alive with a current of "what the hell did we do?" What I wouldn't have given to read their minds, but, by the same token, I wasn't sure I wanted to know.

I didn't ask. They didn't say. One by one, we went our separate ways, getting ready to go and making quick escapes to our respective daily routines.

On my way to work, I wondered how this would end. Would we all just ignore it until we came to an unspoken agreement that it never happened, then move on? Would everything be back to normal tonight?

Whatever the case, I wasn't going to be concentrating on anything else any time soon. This had to be resolved, and soon.

If nothing else, maybe Ethan's trip to Canada later in the week would give me a chance to get back on the same page with Kieran. I could deal with Ethan when he returned, but maybe a few days without him would be enough to kill some of this awkwardness with Kieran.

Ethan left for Toronto on Thursday morning. When I came home from work, Kieran was already gone for an evening shift, so I had the house to myself.

After I'd worked out, showered and changed clothes, I went about making myself some dinner, but I was restless. Unsettled.

To drown out the silence while I cooked, I put on some

music. It helped a little, but after a while, even that wasn't enough. Eventually, the music got annoying. In fact, it got intrusive, like someone trying to talk to me while I was having a conversation with someone else, so I clicked off the radio and tried to ignore the silence that demanded my full attention.

Without the music, I was more acutely aware of the cold emptiness that filled the house. It was a strange feeling, something completely alien. I'd had the house to myself more than a few times in the past, but this was different somehow.

"You're being ridiculous," I muttered as I cleaned up the kitchen. Ethan had gone away on business before. Sometimes his trips coincided with Sabrina's trips to Portland to stay with her mother, so I'd have the house to myself for days at a time. I always preferred company, but I was also perfectly comfortable being alone.

I could handle Sabrina and Ethan being out of the house even when, if given the choice, I'd rather have them around. So why couldn't I deal with him being gone when that's exactly where I wanted him to be?

With a sick feeling, I put two and two together. This was different because it was a sample of life without Ethan. He wasn't coming home tonight. Sooner or later, he wouldn't be coming home at all. That day couldn't come soon enough, so, by all rights, I should have been relieved to have a break from him for a few days.

Then another penny dropped. I didn't like this because I couldn't settle into it. He'd be home in a few days, before I could get used to him being gone, so I wasn't letting myself get used to it.

I rubbed my eyes and groaned with frustration. This long, drawn-out breakup was driving me insane. The anticipation of the end, this feeling of everything being up in the air, just needed to be over. I needed him gone so I could finish getting over him.

I was halfway through my second DVD of the evening—watching *American Beauty* for the millionth time—when Kieran came home from work.

When he came into the living room, I paused the movie and looked up.

"You're up late," he said.

I shrugged. "Couldn't sleep."

He muffled a nervous cough with his hand. "So, just staying up late watching movies?"

I nodded. "Yeah. Wasn't much else to do."

He avoided my eyes, but didn't walk away. The silence waited for us to fill it with small talk. Something. Anything. I hesitated to speak, because the one thing I wanted to say was the one thing I wasn't sure he wanted to hear. This was the first time we'd spoken since the night of the threesome. We certainly hadn't touched. I wasn't sure if he regretted it or not, but I needed to know, one way or the other.

And I could think of only one way to be sure, but hell if I knew how to suggest it.

I cleared my throat. "Ethan's out of town."

"I know. He mentioned he was going to, what, Canada?"

"Toronto. He has a job interview there."

"Oh."

I swallowed hard. "Which leaves us with the house to ourselves." I looked him in the eye in spite of my nervousness. "No one to hear a thing, no one to walk in on us."

His expression was completely unreadable. For a long moment, he was silent. Then he said, "I've been at work all night." His gaze darted down the hall and back before meeting mine again. "I could use a shower."

My heart pounded. "Is that an invitation?"

"That depends." He pulled at the edge of his bowtie, the quick, simple motion reducing the flawless bow to a single strip of black. "Are you accepting?"

Chapter Twenty-two

As soon as we were in the shower, any regrets or concerns or inhibitions we might have had were gone.

Kieran slammed me up against the tile wall, kissing me deeply and desperately. We both clawed at each other, grasping shoulders and hair and hips, anything that would keep the other from pulling away.

"I can't wait," he said, panting against my mouth. "I, fuck—" He kissed me again, damn near pulling the air out of my lungs. When he broke the kiss this time, he reached for the condoms and lube we'd brought in with us. "I can't wait."

I shivered and kissed his neck while he put on the condom. His voice thrummed beneath the five o'clock shadow on his throat, simultaneously coarse and ticklish against my lips.

"Turn around," he growled. When I did, he pushed my legs apart with his knee and, before I could even shiver with anticipation, his cock was against me, then inside me.

"Holy fuck," I whispered, closing my eyes as his strokes became deep, hard thrusts.

"Like that?" He sounded like he was speaking through clenched teeth.

"God, yes, that's..." I trailed off, forgetting what language I spoke as he blurred the line between pain and pleasure. I couldn't even hear the rushing water anymore, not over the sound of my own feeble attempts to articulate how good this felt and how much more I wanted.

He panted against my shoulder. "That feels fucking perfect," he slurred. "You feel so, so, fucking..." Shuddering against me, he moaned through what must have been chattering teeth. Then his spine straightened and he gasped, his cock twitching inside me, and a second later he released a throaty roar and came.

My knees almost gave out as he withdrew slowly, as if his body against mine was the only thing keeping me from sinking to the floor. So turned on, so fucking turned on, so close to losing it...

"Turn around," he said. It was a plea this time, not the growled command from earlier. When I did, his body was against mine once again, leaning me against the wall and kissing me passionately. His fingers trailed down my side, and he drew his hips back just enough to allow his hand between us. When he stroked my cock, I gasped, breaking the kiss, and he went to his knees.

I heard myself moan before I even realized I was doing it. Had it not been for the wall behind me, I definitely would have collapsed. As it was, I thought my spine was going to melt from the incredible things that man did with his mouth. Swirling his tongue here, deep-throating there, then fluttering the tip of his tongue in *just* the right places.

I couldn't have lasted if I tried, and I didn't try. I gave in completely, letting him work his magic. It wasn't long before a perfectly timed circle of his tongue around the head of my cock put me right on the edge.

"Fuck, don't stop, Kieran, don't stop," I moaned. "Don't...stop...don't..."

He didn't stop. He took my cock deeper, fluttered his tongue faster, circled, swirled, stroked, but it was the low moan of pleasure—*his* pleasure—from the back of his throat, vibrating against my hypersensitive skin, that made my vision turn white.

When he rose, we were both shaking. He put his arms around me and we held each other up as he kissed me with my own semen on his tongue. Together, we took a step away from the wall and let the water rush over both of us, washing away the sweat and tremors. Our hands were all over each other, simply touching for the sake of touching, hot hands against hot skin beneath hot water.

How long we stood like that, lazily kissing and touching, I couldn't say. Eventually, though, I caught my breath enough to speak.

I combed my fingers through his hair and kissed him gently. "You did all the work this time."

He smiled, running his tongue across the inside of his lip. "I wouldn't call that work."

"You know what I mean." I dipped my head and kissed his neck. "I think I owe you."

"Please," he murmured, letting his head fall back to give me more access to his throat. "Like you never do anything for me."

"No, I insist."

"Well in that case," Kieran reached past me and turned off the shower. "Don't let me stop you."

Chapter Twenty-three

Lying in his bed, Kieran rested his head on my chest. His hair was still damp as much from the shower as from sweat as I absently ran my fingers through it. With my other hand, I rubbed my eyes. Neither of us spoke.

Ah, there you are, awkward silence. We're becoming rather well-acquainted, aren't we?

Several minutes passed, and the quiet didn't get any more comfortable. Finally, Kieran spoke.

"Okay, I have to know," he said. "What the hell happened the other night?"

"What do you mean? Or, I guess I should ask, which part?"

"When Ethan walked in, neither of you missed a beat."

I shrugged. "Neither did you."

"Well, no. It was hot. I wasn't really thinking much of anything except that watching the two of you turned me on." He laughed shyly. "Kind of difficult to think when I'm watching two guys make out while I'm sucking one's cock, you know?"

I laughed. "Yeah, I can imagine."

Kieran turned over onto his stomach and held himself up on his forearms. "It wasn't until later, that it occurred to me, aren't you two *ex*-boyfriends?"

"And you've never had ex sex before?"

"Okay, you've got me there. I just didn't think you two..."

"Actually, we've pretty much settled things. We had a good long talk and—" I couldn't help but chuckle. "Well, let's just say we figured out that we always got along better when we were still sleeping together."

He blinked. "So, you guys, you're—" He shook his head, then looked at me again. "You're back together?"

"No, no, not back together. Well, in the physical sense, I guess we are, but it's just something casual. No commitment. Kind of a..." I trailed off, trying to find the most apt description.

He grinned. "Ex-boyfriends with benefits?"

I laughed. "Yes, exactly." In the back of my mind, I still couldn't shake my concerns about exactly where I stood with Ethan now, but that could be dealt with when he returned from Canada. For the moment, I was content to put the awkwardness with Kieran aside.

"Well, I guess that pretty much takes care everything I was worried about. Wouldn't that be something to tell my parents next time they call to see how I'm doing?" He shook his head. "Hey, Mom, I'm fucking both my roommates, and they're fucking each other, so, hello? Hello?"

We both laughed aloud.

Then he fell silent, his eyes appearing to lose focus as a pair of deep grooves formed between his eyebrows.

"What?" I asked.

"I was just thinking." He paused, swallowing. "Are you guys—" Another pause. "Is there any chance of the two of you, you know, getting back together?"

"Oh God, no."

His eyebrows jumped and he cocked his head. "Really?"

"Absolutely. Sex is one thing. He and I..." I shook my head.

135

"No. Why?"

He shrugged. "I was just curious. Seemed like lately, even before the other night, you two have been…"

"What?"

"I don't know. Closer?"

"If by closer you mean we aren't ready to kill each other, sure. But we're a long way from where we used to be." *And there's no going back down that road, even if I wanted to.*

"And it…" He paused again, furrowing his brow before casting me a cautious look. "It doesn't bother you two at all, that you're both sleeping with me?"

"If it did," I said, running my fingers through his hair, "the other night never would have happened." *And I'm still not sure it should have. This, I can do. That, I'm not sure.*

"In that case…" Kieran moved a little closer, letting his fingertips drift across my chest, then down.

"You're insatiable," I said, grinning just before I kissed him.

"Is that a problem?" He dipped his head to kiss my neck as his hand closed around my cock and stroked gently.

I put my arms around him. "Not a problem at all."

Chapter Twenty-four

"Dad?"

I jumped, raising my eyes to meet Sabrina's from across the café table. "Hmm? Sorry, I—"

"You were zoning out." She laughed tentatively. "You okay?"

I nodded and reached for the coffee I'd barely touched. "I'm fine. Just, you know, spacing out." I sipped my coffee, which had gone cold. "I'm sorry, what were you saying?"

She sighed and rolled her eyes. "I said I met a musician, he's doing my tattoos in his basement, and I'm having his baby."

"Very funny." I rubbed the back of my neck and sighed. "I'm sorry, baby, it's just been one of those days."

"Dad, seriously, you're out of it tonight. Are—" She bit her lip. "Things with Ethan?"

My shoulders slumped under the weight of his name and the worry in her voice. "Yeah, but..." I gestured dismissively. "Nothing you need to worry about."

She raised an eyebrow. "But I will, whether or not you give me permission to."

"Sabrina, it's between—"

"Dad, I can handle it. It's not like I don't know what's going on."

Oh, trust me, sweetheart, you have no idea. I rubbed the bridge of my nose and sighed again.

"Dad, just tell me. I can handle it. I'm not a kid anymore."

"You're still *my* kid, and I'm not going to dump all of this on you." I leaned forward, folding my hands and resting my forearms on the edge of the table. "Listen, you know what it's like to break up with someone, don't you?"

"Yes, I have. It sucks."

"Okay, so you know it's never easy, right?"

"Sure." She shrugged. "But the longest I've ever been with someone is a year. You're breaking up with someone after a freaking *decade*."

I narrowly avoided flinching enough to let her see it. "Even still, it's the same idea. It's never easy. It's not fun." *And my God, are we making things more complicated than they need to be.* I cleared my throat. "And after this long, it's bound to, well, suck."

"Was it this bad when you and Mom broke up?"

That time, I couldn't hide the flinch. I stared into my coffee cup and let out a breath. "That was..." I paused. "Different."

"How?"

"Well..." I sat back, tapping my thumbs on the side of my coffee cup. *I never had to keep living with her after we called it off. I never shared another lover with her. I never loved her like I loved—* I cleared my throat again. "You know, it probably was the same. It's just been so long." I forced a smile. "Ask me again in about ten years."

She laughed half-heartedly. "I just hate seeing you both like this."

"I know. And I hate dragging you through it with us. It's just...one of this things."

"But are—"

I put my hand up, shaking my head. "Sabrina, I'm not dumping this on you."

"I'm *asking* you," she said. "Are you okay with it? Because I don't think you are."

I eyed her. "Oh? And why not?"

She shrugged, but held my gaze with a look of stubborn certainty that made her a mirror image of her mother. Ticking points off on her fingers, she said, "Because you've been spacing out all night. And any time I bring up his name, you look like someone just slapped you across the face. And when I mention—"

"Okay, I get it." I put my hands up. "I get it."

"So am I right?"

I steepled my fingers in front of my lips and sighed. I thought I was okay with this. I'd long ago gotten over the sting of Ethan saying goodbye, and now I just wanted him gone. I'd agreed to our casual arrangement because it kept the peace and, as he'd pointed out, we did get along better when we were still sleeping together. I was *not* still hung up on him.

"Dad?"

"I'm fine." *Am I?* "Really."

She looked away for a moment, then picked up her coffee cup in both hands, resting her elbows on the table. She raised it to her lips, then stopped. Without taking a sip, she set it back on the saucer and looked at me. "Is Ethan really moving to Toronto?"

I wanted to groan at the thought, but didn't. I wanted to convince myself the knot in my stomach was just because of the cold coffee I'd drunk, but couldn't. Taking a breath, I said, "I think so. He went there for an interview. Just got back this afternoon, in fact." I let out a breath. "So, I think they're serious about hiring him."

Her shoulders dropped a little.

"I'm so sorry, baby," I said. "I know this is hard for you."

She shrugged. Sniffed sharply. Smiled, though it didn't quite make it to her eyes. "Well, like you said, it's just one of those things."

"Yeah," I said dryly. "One of those things." I picked up my coffee and took a drink. It tasted horrible now that it was cold, but it was better than a dry mouth.

She cleared her throat and took a breath as she squared her shoulders. Quintessential Sabrina: Not fighting it, just adapting to it, no matter how much it obviously hurt. I envied her for that, especially now, because this conversation was killing me.

She looked me in the eye. "So if he takes this job, does our deal still stand about plane tickets?"

"Absolutely." Then I chanced a grin. "Well, as long as you keep your grades up."

She tried to look upset, but the upturned corner of her mouth betrayed the façade. "What? That wasn't part of the deal."

"That was before I saw your history grade." I gave her a pointed look.

She laughed softly and dropped her gaze, but when she looked at me again, the humor was gone. "You'll really pay for me to go see him?"

"Sabrina, I won't keep you from him. Grades or not, the deal still stands. You two set it up, I'll buy the ticket."

That restored her smile. "I don't have to keep my grades up, then?"

I gave her my least convincing look of disapproval. "Don't push it."

She grinned. "So have you thought about meeting anyone new?"

Christ, you really do know how to pick up and move on, don't you? "Not yet, and no I don't want to meet anyone from your dorm."

"Actually, I do have this incredibly hot math professor, and—"

"Sabrina!"

She put her hands up. "What? I think he could be your type."

"And what type is that?"

She shrugged. "Old."

"Oh, shut up." I laughed, rolling my eyes.

"Hey, don't knock him 'til you try him," she said with a knowing smirk.

I raised my eyebrows. "Sabrina..."

"No, I have not tried him. Jesus, Dad." She wrinkled her nose. "I wouldn't go after something that old." She set down her coffee cup and gestured dismissively. "Don't worry, I'm pretty sure he bats for your team."

I rolled my eyes. "I'm not even going to ask how you know that."

After we'd eaten, I dropped Sabrina off at her dorm.

"So, are you sure you're okay?" she asked before she got out of the car.

Far from it, baby. "I'm fine. Now get in there and finish

studying."

She gave a theatrical sigh and rolled her eyes, then hugged me. "Good night. I love you."

"Love you too."

After she'd gone inside, I pulled out of the parking lot and headed home. On the way back to Capitol Hill, I couldn't get our conversation out of my mind. As much as I'd wanted to keep this out of her sight, I should have known she would pick up on it. She'd always known when Ethan and I were at odds. Hell, even as a toddler, she always seemed to know when her mother and I weren't getting along. It shouldn't have surprised me that she'd know this was all bothering me this much. And really, it didn't.

It surprised me that it *was* bothering me this much.

Chapter Twenty-five

Footsteps and voices past my bedroom door nearly made me groan aloud. I hoped they would go into Kieran's room, but one of the floorboards on the stairs squeaked, then another. *Please, no, not tonight.*

Overhearing them was even worse now that I knew exactly what they looked like together. I had been a part of everything they did now, had been right there when the bed creaked this way or Kieran moaned that way. Every sound was amplified because I knew. The whole damned house seemed to shift and settle to accommodate them or taunt me. Or both.

One more creak of that bed, and I was going to lose my mind. I grabbed my jacket and keys and headed down to the garage.

As I backed out of the garage, I called Dale.

"Isn't it past your bedtime?" he asked when he answered.

"Shut up." I laughed. "You up for a beer? I'll buy."

"Free booze? Oh, tell me when and where, my friend."

I chuckled. "Meet me at The Lucky Seven."

"On my way."

The Lucky Seven was a neon-and-jukebox tavern a few blocks south of Capitol Hill. Since it was a weeknight and any major sporting events were over for the night, the place was deserted. Deserted and quiet.

Not that I cared. It could be noisy as hell as long as it didn't sound like groans and bedsprings.

I grabbed a seat at the bar and ordered myself one of the local microbrews while I waited for Dale. Fortunately, I didn't have to be alone with my thoughts for long. When there was free alcohol on the line, Dale always arrived in very short order.

"So what's going on?" he said as he materialized beside me. "Trouble with the harem?"

I raised an eyebrow. "Harem?"

He shrugged. "Fuck buddies? Playthings? Man toys?"

I managed a laugh. "Yeah, something like that."

"So, whatever they are, I assume they're causing problems?" He looked around. "And where the hell's my beer?"

I chuckled and shook my head. "I was just waiting until you got here so it would still be cold." I flagged down the bartender, and Dale ordered. After I'd paid and Dale was happily sipping a Killian's Red, I said, "And yes, you're right, they're the problem tonight."

"So what are they doing? Obviously not you, since you're here."

I glared at him. Then I rolled my eyes. "Each other." I paused to sip my beer. "And I got tired of hearing it."

"I can't blame you there. I mean, it's gotta be hot, I'm sure Ethan's a scream—" My pointed glare cut him off. He quickly said, "Anyway, that has to be weird. Especially if you're doing both of them too."

"And especially after I've done them at the same time."

"What?!" Dale huffed and shook his head. "Christ on a bike, Rhett, I wish I had your problems."

"No you don't, trust me." I sighed and rubbed my eyes. "I just wish this whole thing was over."

"So you want him gone, even though you're fucking him?"

"I'm fucking him because it makes it easier to put up with him," I growled into my beer bottle.

"So it has nothing to do with wanting him?" He raised an eyebrow and gave me his patented look of skepticism. "You're just suffering through it to pass the time?"

I let out a breath. "No, not quite," I admitted. "Don't get me wrong, the sex is incredible. Probably some of the best we've ever had. It's just..."

"It's just what?"

I didn't speak for a moment, quietly watching my fingers peel the label on my beer bottle. Finally, I said, "This is going to sound crazy, but you know when he was in Toronto last week?" I exhaled hard. "I missed him. I fucking missed him." I took a long swallow of beer. "And the minute he got home? I wanted him gone."

Dale rolled his eyes. "Well, do you miss him or do you want him gone?"

I rubbed my forehead. "Fuck, I don't know. It's like, once he was home, I was pissed at him for being gone. I just, I'd..."

"Gotten used to him being gone?"

"No, not at all, I—" I paused. "Hell, I don't know. But when he got home, I didn't want him anywhere near me. On one hand, I wanted to drag him to bed and make up for the last few days. On the other, I wanted him to just *leave*. It was like I was repulsed by him and wanted him and hated him and—"

"Rhett, Rhett, slow down." Dale put up his hands. "Have

you guys talked at all?"

"About what?"

He let out a disgusted breath. "About anything other than how much you like fucking your roommate? Jesus, Rhett. Listen, maybe you guys need to sit down and talk. Maybe there's something, I don't know, unresolved."

"The only thing unresolved is the fact that my ex-boyfriend and I still live together," I muttered. "The sooner he's gone—"

"Which explains why you missed him while he was in Toronto, right?"

I rested my forehead in my hand and closed my eyes. "None of it makes any sense, Dale. I'm not even sure if I missed him, or if I wanted him gone, or what. All I know is that I'm fucking exhausted."

"You just want to be done breaking up with him."

I nodded. "Yeah, that's basically it. Either stay or go, but fucking do—"

"Whoa, whoa, whoa." Dale slammed his beer down hard enough to startle us both. "Since when is staying an option?"

My heart skipped, but I quickly waved the thought away with a sharp gesture. "That's not what I meant. I mean, I just want it over. Sooner than later. This bullshit is driving me insane."

"So you want him to go, then?" Dale asked. "Not stick around if he so desires?"

I stared at my drink, watching flickering neon light play along the edges of the brown glass. "Yes, I want him to go."

"Rhett, look at me," Dale ordered. When I did, he said, "Look me in the eye and tell me that you don't want Ethan back."

I looked him in the eye, opened my mouth to speak, but the

words wouldn't come. Then I sighed and shook my head. "Dale, even if I did want him back—"

"Which you do."

I glared at him. "Even if I *did*, which I do *not*, that doesn't change the fact that he ended things. He dumped me, remember?"

"True." He shrugged. "But since you want—"

"I do not want him back," I growled. "I want him gone. And, like I said, he obviously doesn't want me back, so what difference would it make if I did want him?"

"Well, it would explain why you can't decide whether or not you miss him," he said. "And why you went scrambling out of the house on a weeknight to spend time with me of all people when you could just as easily have put on some headphones until they were done."

My beer bottle stopped just shy of my lips. He had a point. My MP3 player had noise-cancelling headphones. I could have drowned the sound out and gone to sleep, or waited until they were done, or—

"See?" He grinned. "I was right."

"No, you're not. I just needed to get away because even if I couldn't hear them, I still knew what they were doing."

"Jealous?"

"Why would I be jealous?" I paused to take a drink. "I'm fucking both of them. What's there to be jealous of?"

Dale raised an eyebrow. "You tell me."

I pulled into the garage and killed the engine. For a long moment, I just sat in the driver's seat, resting my elbow below the window and rubbing the bridge of my nose. Ethan and

Kieran were most likely asleep, but I just couldn't bring myself to go inside yet.

What the hell is wrong with me?

I wasn't jealous. No matter how much Dale had tried to convince me otherwise, I wasn't jealous and had no reason to be. This was just casual sex, and I could do casual sex. I'd done it in the past, and I could do it with Kieran without batting an eye. Love and sex weren't indivisible, and I could easily have one without the other.

And I could deal with Kieran and Ethan sleeping together. Tonight, I didn't feel like listening to it, but I could deal with it. Couldn't I?

Then the chill of enlightenment raised the hairs on the back of my neck. Maybe it wasn't the fact that Ethan and Kieran were having sex that bothered me. Maybe it was the fact that I was having sex with them. Specifically, Ethan.

It was hot. There was no sense even trying to deny that. Physically, it was some of the hottest sex I'd ever experienced.

But something was missing.

Or, more accurately, something was *there*: distance. No matter how close I got to him physically, I could neither close nor deny the distance between us.

With or without Kieran, sex with Ethan was a taste of the past. Of the days before the cold, bitter void had settled in between us. A glance at intimacy long forgotten. Sex with him was addictive because it was all we had left that wasn't tainted by our separation, but every time it ended, it only served to emphasize how far apart we were. That brief taste of something good made the cold colder, the quiet quieter, and the bitterness bitterer.

And I couldn't do it anymore.

I had to end this arrangement with Ethan. No matter how hot it was, it couldn't go on because I couldn't stand the cold.

Chapter Twenty-six

When I finally had the opportunity to talk to Ethan, when we were both home at a reasonable hour and had the house to ourselves for an evening, nerves got the best of me. I avoided him like the plague.

He caught up to me, though. In the kitchen, where we seemed to argue more than anywhere else in the house, he stood in the doorway and glared at me.

"What the hell is going on?" he asked.

I looked up. "What?"

He rolled his eyes. "Before I left for Toronto, we were fucking like crazy. Then I got the cold shoulder after that threesome, but figured whatever it was, you'd get over it. Now I'm back and you're still giving me the cold shoulder." He put his hands up. "So what the hell did I do?" His lips twisted into a scowl and his eyebrows demanded an answer.

"So I'm the only one who was giving the cold shoulder after that night?" I snapped. "Seems to me that no one was talking the next morning."

"Well, after last night—" His scowl turned into a sarcastic smirk. "Obviously Kieran is okay with me. And I'm quite all right with him, thanks for asking, so—" He put his hands up again. "That just leaves the two of us."

I gritted my teeth. "I guess it does."

Folding his arms across his chest, he rested his hip against the counter. "So, what's the fucking problem?"

I took a deep breath, but the words didn't come. This was the opportunity I was waiting for, so why couldn't I say it?

He exhaled hard. "Or are we just going to stand here in silence like—"

"Maybe I'm having a hard time with this 'broken up but still together' shit."

"We're not still together." He shrugged. "This is just sex."

I shifted my weight. "Okay, so maybe it's a bit weird having 'just sex' with someone who I can barely have a civil conversation with outside the bedroom." *Especially when the sex is so, so good and the rest of the time we're like this.*

"Well, we've tried our damndest to get along, and it didn't work. So we can either fuck in between not getting along, or we can just not get along." He shrugged again. "Sleeping together seems like the lesser of two evils to me."

I rolled my eyes. "Ever the eloquent one."

He folded his arms across his chest and narrowed his eyes. "Do you have any better ideas? Because you're just as stuck in this situation as I am."

"What do you want me to say, Ethan?" I said. "This isn't easy. This isn't...fuck, I don't know what the word is. Normal? Comfortable?"

"No, it's not. But it is what it is."

"Yeah, I know. The thing is, it's...I..." I cursed under my breath, searching for the words.

"Being together wasn't easy, either," he said, his voice gentler.

But was being together ever this hard? "No, it wasn't, but

151

knowing that doesn't make separating any easier. There's nothing simple about any of this."

"I know." He sighed and ran a hand through his hair. "I don't think either of us expected it to be."

"Did you expect splitting up to be this complicated?"

He shook his head. "No. But I never imagined it would be easy."

Silence again. That familiar maddening silence that I just couldn't get used to. It was tempting just to curse in frustration, but that would only serve to emphasize the subsequent quiet.

I'd come into this conversation with every intention of putting some more distance between us, breaking that last tie of intimacy that made this that much less bearable, but...what was I supposed to say?

"By the way, as long as we're talking about how much this sucks, I don't want to sleep with you anymore."

"Speaking of uncomfortable subjects..."

"Fuck me. No, no, I mean, fuck you. Fuck you for being gone and still being here."

My stomach turned. My damned divorce hadn't been this complicated.

Ethan tapped his fingers on the counter then he ran a hand through his hair and looked me in the eye. "Look, we—" He closed his eyes, exhaling sharply. "This—" He cursed under his breath and dropped his gaze.

I waited, unsure what it was he wanted to say and completely at a loss for how to fill this silence.

All at once, he shifted his weight, let out a sharp breath. "Do you want to fuck?"

With a cough of laughter, I said, "What? Are you—"

"It beats the hell out of this." He looked equal parts nervous and irritated.

"Yeah, but this isn't exactly what I'd call foreplay," I growled.

"And maybe it'll be easier to talk after we've both released a bit of tension, don't you think?"

I stared at him. "You're serious. All of this shit, all of this, all—" I paused, shaking my head. "And you're suddenly in the mood to fuck?"

His face colored a little, and he set his jaw as he avoided my eyes. "I can't say I am. But I'm sure as hell not in the mood to fight."

I pressed my fingers into the bridge of my nose. Christ, he hadn't changed a bit. When we were still together, we could go days on end without speaking, and he wouldn't miss a night of trying to initiate sex. It didn't matter how horny I was; I had my limits.

But I wanted him. It didn't matter how wrong it was, I wanted him. And I hated him for making it that much more difficult for me to pull away.

Before I could speak, Ethan said, "Look, Rhett, we live in the same house. Whatever happened is in the past. I'm not going to pretend I'm not still attracted to you. And for that matter, we always did get along better when we were still fucking."

"So you're suggesting we keep sleeping together just to keep the peace?"

The half-grin that spread across his lips was as mischievous as it was cautious. "Well, I never said I didn't enjoy it. It just has the added benefit of maintaining harmony in the house too." Then the grin fell, and he shrugged. "Maybe if we—" The color in his cheeks darkened even more. "You know what,

153

forget I mentioned it." He started to leave.

"Wait," I said.

He stopped in his tracks, looking at me with a mix of anger and embarrassment.

I swallowed. "You are serious, aren't you? About—" I chewed my lip.

"About fucking instead of fighting?" he said, barely whispering. "Yeah. Yeah, I am."

Pushing the self-loathing to the back of my mind, I said, "It doesn't bother you at all, going to bed even with all of this unresolved shit?"

He dropped his gaze and pursed his lips. Then he raised his eyes. "Listen, with the way things are now, every time I look at you..." He paused, hesitating for a moment. Then he took a breath and squared his shoulders. "Every time I look at you, I'm either so pissed I can't stand the sight of you or so fucking horny I can't take my eyes off you. I don't think I have to tell you which I prefer."

I swallowed. "So which is it now?"

"I'm looking at you, aren't I?"

Chapter Twenty-seven

I pulled Ethan onto the bed by his shirt. He offered no resistance. In fact, he damn near threw me down even as I dragged him down. His kiss was frantic, bordering on violent, his stubble brushing roughly against my skin and his tongue demanding access to mine.

Sharp hisses of breath. The bed shifting beneath us. Clothes rustling. Belts jingling. Shoes thumping onto the floor beside the bed. We didn't speak because there was nothing that could be said that was more pressing than our need to touch each other. *This* silence I could deal with.

With every article of clothing we threw aside, we changed position. He rolled onto his back, taking me with him, and forced my shirt up and off. When he went for my belt, I pulled him upright and got rid of his shirt too. As we fumbled with belts and zippers, struggling out of jeans and boxers, we fought for dominance. He was in control, then I was. I was in control, then he was. Whatever anger and bitterness lingered from our conversation in the kitchen came out in every kiss, every growl, every touch. There was no intimacy or affection, just raw desperation and brute strength.

And the more he kissed me like that and dug his fingers into my skin and fought me for control, the more I needed him. Forget foreplay. Getting out of our clothes and trying to gain control was foreplay aplenty, I needed him *now*.

He must have been thinking the same thing, because we both lunged for the stash of condoms at the same time. I beat him to it and grabbed one off the nightstand.

Tearing the wrapper, I said, "Get on your knees."

He didn't hesitate. As I knelt behind him, grasping his hips, the bedcovers bunched in his hands, tension rippling up his forearms and culminating in a shiver that came down his spine and right into my hands. When I pressed my cock against him, he shivered again but quickly relaxed, his fingers releasing the comforter.

I pushed all the way in, withdrew, then did it again, picking up speed with every stroke. I watched myself fucking him, letting the sight of my cock slamming into him again and again completely mesmerize me. The more I watched, the more I wanted, and the closer I got to losing it completely.

And for once, it didn't matter that it was Ethan. I wanted this—the sweat, the pleasure, the orgasm that built with every thrust—whether it was with Ethan, Kieran, or anyone else.

Yes, this is right.

His hips rocked back against mine, matching my rhythm and drawing me deeper inside him.

Yes, I can do this.

"Holy shit, that feels good," he moaned.

Yes, you feel so fucking good, oh God, oh God...

"Oh God, yes," I groaned, my eyes rolling back as electricity shot up my spine. And still it built, the rising tension and deepening ache, approaching the point of unbearable, reaching that point, passing it, and finally I could hold back no longer. I pulled his hips against me, forcing my cock as deep inside him as I could, and came.

As my orgasm subsided, he lowered himself all the way to the bed, and I followed, unable to hold myself up until the trembling stopped. Resting my weight on my forearm, I pulled out slowly.

His muscles quivered as he shifted slightly, and I couldn't resist kissing between his shoulder blades. He inhaled sharply, arching his back against me.

"I want to fuck you," he said in a half-growl, half-whisper.

I nipped the side of his neck. "How do you want me?"

He sucked a breath in through his teeth as goose bumps spread across his skin from the place my lips brushed when I spoke. He started to push himself up, but I stayed over him.

"Tell me." I deliberately let my five o'clock shadow graze the ridge of his shoulder blade.

He shivered again. "On your back."

"Bet you *would* like that, wouldn't you?" I whispered, making a slow circle on his spine with the tip of my tongue.

"Yes, I would," he growled. "*Move.*"

I did, lifting myself off him so he could get a condom and I could get rid of mine. When he rejoined me on the bed, I sat up and kissed him. He tried to lay me back, but I didn't let him. If he wanted it, he was going to have to—

In a heartbeat, he had me flat on my back. "I said," he whispered. "On. Your. Back." And he kissed me again, deeply, angrily, violently. I barely kept myself from moaning; I loved it when he was like this.

"Stay just like that." He sat up slowly, keeping his hands on my sides and eyeing me as if he thought I'd try to shift positions again. Evidently certain I was going to stay still, he ran his hands down to my sides and onto my hips.

Guiding himself with one hand, steadying me with the

other, he pushed in slowly. As he slid deeper, his lips parted and his eyes closed. Then his head fell back as he released a low moan. "Oh God..." His voice sounded choked, like someone on the verge of tears or insanity. "Oh God, that's..." His breath caught as he withdrew, then pushed in again.

A shudder ran up my spine, and my hips shifted a little. He must have thought I was trying to move, because he suddenly grabbed my wrists and pinned my arms beside my head on the pillow. Holding me down with both his weight and the sheer magnitude of his presence, he kissed me hard. My hands closed into tight, trembling, frustrated fists. He felt so good, he tasted so good, but I couldn't touch him. The more he kissed me and fucked me, the more I wanted to touch him, but he kept my arms immobile.

Breaking the kiss with a gasp, he pushed himself up and, using his grip on my arms as leverage, drove himself deeper. Sweat rolled down his temples and exertion tightened his lips to the point he almost bared his teeth.

All the while, he stared down at me and I stared right back up at him. And for the first time, I felt nothing. No anger, no longing, *nothing*. All that existed was the physical pleasure-almost-pain as Ethan fucked me harder and harder. Every thrust he took emphasized what we were and what we were not.

This is all we are. Slam. *Lovers, nothing more.* Slam. *Lovers, nothing less.* Slam. *Fucking, not making love.*

Finally, it was just sex. Casual sex for the sake of an orgasm or two and peace in the house. The passionate heat ended with our bodies. Everything else was cold, dead, and gone.

"Oh...fuck..." he moaned, closing his eyes as a tremor interrupted his rhythm. "Oh fuck, I'm gonna..." Another moan, just this side of a completely surrendered whimper. I rocked my hips in time with his now uneven thrusts, and he released a throaty roar as his spine straightened, then arched, then collapsed.

His head fell beside mine, shoulders rising and falling as he panted, each exhalation a cool gust across my perspiration-dampened skin.

When he finally pushed himself up, pausing to make sure his arms would really hold him, he stood and took care of the condom. Then we both lay on our backs, not touching, not talking, just breathing.

For once, I didn't feel the need to get closer to him. We'd both gotten what we wanted. I didn't need reassurance that he was still here, because I knew he wasn't.

And, more than I'd thought possible before we stepped into this room tonight, I knew I could live with that.

Never in my life had I been so relieved to be so far from him. This was how it was supposed to be. I could do this after all.

Chapter Twenty-eight

Lying beside him in my bed, we may as well have been on separate floors, but I was relieved. Comfortable. Maybe I was capable of separating my feelings that were from my lust that still was.

Ethan drew a breath and rolled onto his side, facing me. We still didn't touch. In fact, his change of position only widened the gap between us, allowing me to draw an even easier breath.

"So now what?" he said.

"You tell me," I said, smirking. "This was your idea."

He laughed. "Well, I feel even less like fighting now."

"Yeah, me too."

"But we have to get out of this bed eventually," he said. "Now's as good a time as any to figure out what happens next."

I swallowed. "I guess we have two choices. Either we keep sleeping together, or we don't."

"What do you think we should do?"

I took a breath. Arguing in the kitchen, I could have answered this question more easily. I'd long since made up my mind and just needed to find the balls to say it. But now I wasn't so sure. I couldn't deal with the close calls, the tantalizing hints of a happier past, but if it stayed like this—

detached, unemotional sex for the sake of sex—then maybe I could.

"Rhett?"

"I think—" But what if it didn't stay like this? What if we couldn't keep things strictly physical? I sighed. "I don't know. I really don't. What about you?"

"I think," he said, "that if we have to live together, I'd rather have a few hot nights with you now and again to make it bearable."

"I guess I can't argue with that."

"And if anything, it'll balance out some of the bullshit that will probably come up, if I know us."

"What do you mean?"

"Well, knowing us, we're going to snipe and argue from time to time. If you think about it, those lows will make the highs that much better, and with everything we're dealing with, I'll take all the highs I can get." He leaned forward and kissed me gently. "We're in this together, whether we like it or not, so we might as well do the best we can to get through it together until we go our separate ways."

I swallowed. "I hadn't thought of it that way."

Smiling, he kissed me again, then settled back onto his side, propping his head up with one arm. After a moment, his smile faded. "What about Kieran?"

"What about him?"

He shrugged. "Well, we're both still sleeping with him, and after the other night..."

"Maybe that night just caught us all off guard," I said. "I mean, up until you walked into the living room, I don't think any of us expected it to happen."

He laughed softly. "No, definitely not."

"Maybe…" I rolled my piercing around on the roof of my mouth. Did I dare? Was it a good idea?

Ethan cocked his head. "What?"

"Do you think…" I paused. "Do you think the other night was a mistake?"

His brow furrowed, then he shook his head. "No. It was a bit unexpected, which is probably why it was awkward the next day, but, no, I wouldn't call it a mistake."

"Would it be a mistake to do it again?"

His eyebrows jumped. "Are you serious?"

I swallowed. "Why not? It was hot, so…" I gave a half shrug.

He smiled. "Hell yeah, I'd do it again."

"Really?"

"Jesus Christ, yes. Twice the cock, what's not to love?"

I laughed and rolled my eyes. "So eloquent, Ethan."

He chuckled, then leaned forward and kissed me lightly. "Talk to Kieran. If he's down with it, tell me when and where."

A hint of nervousness settled in my chest, but I nodded anyway and slid my arm around his waist. "And between now and then?"

With the tip of his tongue, he slowly moistened his lips just before they curled into that mouthwatering smirk. "I guess it's just the two of us."

Chapter Twenty-nine

Over the next few days, I tried to find an opportunity to broach the subject of another threesome to Kieran. It didn't seem like something we should discuss when one of us was running out the door to work, and that seemed to be the only time we saw each other that week.

One afternoon, though, my opportunity came in the form of an open door. Specifically, the door that was open when I walked past our shared bathroom while Kieran was shaving.

I was two or three steps past before I stopped in my tracks, wondering if I dared. My mind tried to come up with a few hasty reasons why this particular moment wasn't the best time to approach him—*he's getting ready for work, he's busy, he's probably not interested*—but I ignored it. It needed to be done.

Pushing my rational objections to the back of my mind, I stepped back and leaned against the doorframe. We made some casual small talk, shooting the breeze about nothing, but I was determined to get this out on the table before I lost my nerve. I had to, and it was now or never. I needed to do this so I could convince myself I only wanted Ethan as much as I wanted Kieran.

And my God, I realized as I watched him shave, *do I want Kieran*. His hair was wet and unruly, just as it always was when he got out of the shower. He wore nothing but a pair of jeans and a few fading marks that were probably from his last encounter with Ethan.

"Working today?" I asked.

"Not for a few hours yet."

I leaned on the doorframe, arms folded across my chest and trying to look somewhat casual and relaxed as we made small talk. Watching him shave made it almost impossible to keep my thoughts in order. The slowly moving razor kept pulling my attention to the ridges of his cheekbones, the subtle hollow of his cheeks and the sharpness of his jaw. The muffled scratch of blade on stubble reminded me of the way his five o'clock shadow brushed against my lips, especially as he drew the blade up the side of his neck, following the curve I'd memorized a hundred times over.

Trying not to stare, I forced myself just to cut to the chase and discuss what I came to discuss. "Listen," I said, clearing my throat. "About the other night..."

His eyes flicked toward mine in the mirror, watching me instead of the razor. "Which night? Do— Oh. Right."

"Yeah. That night."

His cheeks darkened a little, and the path of the blade once again held his attention and mine. "What about it?"

I swallowed. There was no sense playing games. "Ethan and I talked about it, and we both wanted to know if you'd be game to do it again."

The razor stopped in midstroke. My eyes shifted up and met the reflection of his.

"Are you serious?" he said.

I nodded.

"Even after..." He trailed off, chewing his lip and looking down as he rinsed the razor, frowning as if that simple task required intense focus.

"After what?"

"Rhett, none of us could even look at each other the next day. I don't want to cause things to get weird between you two."

I laughed. "Things have been weird between us since long before you moved in."

"I know, and I don't know that I want to be in the middle of it."

"Understood. But he and I have settled our differences. We had a good long talk a few nights ago about everything. With you, with us, all of that."

"Good to hear," he said, sounding non-committal. He turned on the faucet and leaned down to rinse his face.

"And one thing we both agreed on was that that night was easily one of the hottest things we've ever experienced."

He looked up, reaching for a hand towel to dry his face. "Seriously?"

I nodded.

He put the towel down and looked in the mirror, running his fingertips across his skin to check for missed spots. Watching his finger trace the edge of his jaw, I couldn't keep myself back anymore.

"Kieran," I said, shouldering myself off the doorframe. I put my hands on his sides, the warmth of his skin making my breath catch. "You have no idea."

Our eyes met in the mirror. He gulped. "But, the other night, it just..." He paused. "It just happened."

"I know." I held his gaze even as I turned to kiss the side of his neck.

He released a soft moan. "But, you guys actually want to plan for it now?"

"Absolutely. This time we can't pretend we didn't mean for it to happen." I just barely touched my lips to his shoulder and paused to breathe him in. "We'll know we all want it to happen, no one is getting caught by surprise." Kissing his shoulder once more, I looked at his reflection. "I don't regret the last time. Do you?"

"I don't—" He shivered. "I don't know if I do or not."

"What is there to regret?" I whispered just below his hair. "You two made me come so many times, I couldn't see straight. And I know you enjoyed it too."

"I enjoyed it," he said. "That doesn't mean it was a good idea. I mean, with the way things are with you two..." He squirmed against me, and his breath caught as I trailed fingertips down his spine.

"Don't worry about us, Kieran. All of that is between Ethan and me. It has nothing to do with you." I kissed just behind his ear, grinning to myself when he shuddered the same way Ethan always did. "He and I disagree on a lot of things, but this is the one thing you won't hear us argue about."

"I'm not going to pretend I don't want to." His breath came in short, shallow gasps as I teased his skin with lips and fingers. "I just don't know if we should. I don't want to cause any disagreements between you two."

"You won't, because this is something we do agree on." My hand snaked around his waist. "We both agree that you are fucking hot." I kissed his shoulder as my hand unfastened the top button of his jeans. "We both agree that fucking you is hot." He sucked in a breath as I drew his zipper down. "And we both love watching each other make you come." I kissed his neck and stroked his cock.

Moaning softly, Kieran braced himself against the counter and let his head fall forward. I couldn't tell if his eyes were open or closed, if it was all too much for him or if he watched my hand on his cock.

"Look up, Kieran," I whispered. "Look in the mirror."

He raised his head, lips parted and eyes half-closed.

"This is what Ethan sees," I said. "This is what he sees when we're all together, and I want him to see it again." Leaning forward, I flicked my tongue along the side of his ear and whispered, "I want him to watch me make you come again."

Closing his eyes, Kieran shuddered and moaned, his cock getting thicker and harder in my hand. Leaning against me and gripping the counter for balance, he came. With a sigh and one last tremor, he slumped over the counter, panting and shaking.

With my hands on his hips, I gently turned him around, leaning him against the counter as I kissed him.

"The choice is yours," I whispered, barely breaking the kiss. "But I'm not going to lie. We both want you like that again."

He shivered again, gasping as if the aftershock of his orgasm had caught him off guard. Then he licked his lips, met my eyes and nodded.

Chapter Thirty

It was a few days before all three of us were home at the same time with nowhere else to be. We found all kinds of reasons to be in separate parts of the house, but we all knew. Well, I knew. I wanted it. I wanted them. Tonight. Now or never. But how to suggest it? Last time was easy. Last time just *happened.*

This time, a move had to be made to not one, but two people. Even though we were all in agreement about this and, judging by the looks that passed between us when we crossed paths in the house, we all wanted it *now*, no one broke the ice. It was just a question of who was finally going to blink and end the three-way staring contest.

They must have been on the same wavelength, because it wasn't long before our coy dance of avoidance converged in a slow migration to the living room. No one spoke, no one touched, but we were on the same ground. It was only a matter of time.

Ethan flipped channels, the constant change from one program to the next giving us something upon which to focus our collective attention, but I doubted any of us were really aware of what was on the screen. When Ethan clicked right past *The Usual Suspects*, one of his all-time favorite films, I knew he wasn't watching.

I couldn't decide if the ball of nerves in my stomach was just anticipation or if I was unsure about this. Was this the best way to prove to myself that I only wanted Ethan the way I wanted Kieran? Was there any other way?

Whether it was or not, the fact remained that I did want both of them and, after having them both at the same time before, I desperately wanted them at the same time again. The only thing hotter than one incredible lover was two at the same time.

I glanced at Kieran. I couldn't quite read him. He was nervous, that much was clear in the way his body shifted on the couch and his eyes shifted from me to Ethan and back. But was it nerves about getting things started, or about doing it at all? He'd been hesitant when I approached the subject, and agreed in the heat of the moment, but did he have cold feet now?

Ethan, on the other hand, kicked back on the sofa, one hand behind his head and the other clicking steadily on the remote. The very picture of being completely at ease. Most likely aware of our nerves and waiting for one of us to initiate things.

Kieran looked at me. Glanced at Ethan, eyebrows lifted. Ethan's eyes darted toward me. I looked at Kieran.

There it was, passing from one of us to the next: the *look*. The three-way dare, the unspoken appeal, the silent "someone just fucking *say it*".

The breath Kieran drew had *I'm about to break the ice* written all over it, and Ethan and I turned in unison just as Kieran said to Ethan, "You have enough condoms upstairs?"

"More than enough," Ethan said. As one, we all stood. No one spoke on the way out of the living room, down the hall and up the stairs.

As we stepped into Ethan's bedroom, Kieran shot me an uncertain glance over his shoulder. I gave him a reassuring smile and put my hands on his hips, pulling him back against me.

"You sure you're okay with this?" I whispered.

His eyes flicked back and forth between Ethan and me, then he smiled. "Sex with two hot guys at once? What's not to love?"

"Well, in that case..." I kissed him lightly. Then he put his arms around my neck and kissed me full-on. Abruptly, he broke the kiss with a shiver and sucked in a sharp breath.

Ethan kissed Kieran's neck again, moving up and down from his jaw to his collar.

When he'd recovered from the startle, Kieran kissed me again, more desperately and passionately than before. *Yes*, his lips and tongue told mine. *I want this.*

Ethan's hands found mine on Kieran's sides and slid up my forearms, raising goose bumps with his light touch. My own inhibitions melted away. Kieran was right: Sex with two of the best lovers I'd ever had. At the same time. What wasn't to love?

Kieran tugged at my shirt, and they both released me so I could take it off. Kieran dipped his head and kissed my neck, and I closed my eyes, letting my head fall back. Even with my eyes closed, I was aware of Ethan moving, coming around behind me.

His lips touched the base of my neck, making me shiver. When he pulled me against him, the fabric of his shirt was vaguely coarse against my back, accenting the softness of his breath and the hardness of his cock.

I turned my head and found Ethan's lips as Kieran kissed his way to my shoulder, tracing the edge of one of my tattoos with his tongue.

"I think," Kieran murmured against my skin. "That we're all

a bit overdressed."

Ethan laughed, pausing to kiss the base of my neck again. "I think you're right." We all shed the last of our clothes and Kieran made his lack of inhibition abundantly clear when he went to his knees. In almost the same instant Kieran's lips were around my cock, Ethan kissed me so passionately, he almost distracted me from what Kieran's mouth and hands were doing.

I moaned into Ethan's kiss, holding his shoulders for balance. Neither of them held back, one kissing me as hungrily as the other sucked my cock. Just as every time they'd done this in the past, their combined efforts drove me out of my mind and right to, then over, the edge. I swore Ethan's kiss was as responsible for my intense, spine-melting orgasm as everything Kieran did to my cock.

"Much more of that, and *I'm* going to come," Kieran said, licking his lips as he stood. "I have got to fuck one of you."

Ethan grinned. "Which one?"

Kieran reached for a condom. "You two decide."

Ethan and I both looked at each other with raised eyebrows. Then he backed toward the bed, pulling me with him, and leaned against it. He kissed me, cupping my face with one hand, then the other. His kiss took my breath away, but not for the reasons I'd expected. It was intense in its slow sensuality, not the desperate hunger I expected. The tenderness of his touch, the gentleness, was out of place in a situation like this, like it was driven by something that didn't belong here.

And it did nothing to convince me that I was capable of having "just sex" with him like I did with Kieran.

I dipped my head and my lips went to his neck, then down his chest and away from his disconcerting kiss.

Kieran's hand rested on the small of my back, and I sucked in a breath when the cool lube on his cock touched my skin. He pushed into me slowly and I, moving just as slowly, deep-throated Ethan.

I want you both. As Kieran fucked me, I devoured Ethan's cock. *I want you both exactly same way, no more or less.* Ethan's fingers twitched in my hair, and he released a low groan. Kieran's hands trembled against my hips and he, too, moaned softly. *Yes, this is how it's supposed to be.*

Above it all, though, a strange feeling found its way into my mind. Everything about this was hot. It was sexual and nothing more, just like it was last time and like it needed to stay, but something was...off.

Out of place.

Imbalanced.

I pushed those thoughts away. It was just nerves. Fear of a repeat of the awkwardness from last time. Or my own inability to separate my past with Ethan from my present with him, which was the very thing I'd hoped to do by having him and Kieran at once. It was the very thing I did more and more every time Kieran thrust inside me and every time I took Ethan's cock as far into my mouth as I could.

I glanced up at Ethan as I ran my tongue along the underside of his cock. He closed his eyes and groaned softly, running his fingers through my hair. Behind me, Kieran released a low growl and thrust deeper, harder. A shiver ran through me and the more Kieran fucked me, the more hungrily I sucked Ethan's cock.

Still, in the back of my mind, I couldn't shake this odd feeling. More than that, I couldn't get past the feeling that this imbalance didn't start or end with me. Did Kieran still have reservations? Or was Ethan—

Kieran tightened his grip on my hips and slammed into me harder, bringing me out of my thoughts and into the present.

"Oh Jesus..." His voice dwindled to a helpless whimper. "Oh my God, oh my fucking God..." His cock twitched inside me, and his fingers dug into my hips. Just when I thought he wouldn't last another second, I swiveled my hips slightly, the way he often did to me, and he roared and shuddered against me.

As Kieran pulled out, I ran my tongue around the head of Ethan's cock, then slowly deep-throated him, just the way I knew he loved it. He moaned and trembled, grasping my hair gently.

"Don't make me come yet. That is so—" He gasped. The fingers running through my hair tightened just slightly, as if they wanted to stop me but couldn't quite bring themselves to do so. Finally, restraint won over desire, and he gently pushed my head back. I looked up and he nodded for me to stand.

"Not yet, not yet," he said as I stood. He kissed me passionately, then murmured, "I still want to be inside you." The promise and desperation in his voice made my breath catch. I hadn't heard him want me like that in ages, and I'd forgotten just how much it turned me on.

He looked past me and nodded to Kieran. Behind me, foil rustled and, a second later, Ethan put his hand up and caught the unopened condom. Tearing the wrapper with his teeth, he said, "Lie on your back."

I smiled and kissed him lightly before doing as he asked. That was one of my favorite ways for him to fuck me anyway, but I was especially thankful for it this time. At least then I wouldn't have to worry about my knees shaking out from under me.

As Ethan rolled the condom on, Kieran poured some lube into his own hand. They caught each other's eyes, and Kieran grinned. He pulled Ethan into a kiss, but Ethan hesitated. For a second, I thought he was resisting Kieran's kiss, but as Kieran's arm and shoulder moved, I realized he was stroking Ethan's cock. It wasn't resistance, just distraction.

What else would it be? Ethan's the least uncertain of the three of us. I shook my head and watched them.

"That's..." Ethan whispered, barely breaking the kiss. "Oh God, that's..." He exhaled hard. "Fuck, I can't wait." They both climbed onto the bed. Ethan leaned down to kiss me quickly, then sat up and pressed his cock against me.

I bit my lip and my back arched as Ethan pushed into me slowly.

"Fucking hell, you feel good," he breathed, exhaling through parted lips as his eyes rolled back.

Kieran knelt behind Ethan and kissed his neck and shoulders. Ethan's entire body responded to every gentle, lingering kiss, shivering and driving his cock deeper inside me. Kieran whispered something in his ear, no doubt something deliciously filthy if his grin was any indication, and Ethan sucked in a breath. When Kieran found that perfect spot behind Ethan's ear, Ethan whimpered and closed his eyes.

"Oh my God, between the two of you," Ethan moaned. He opened his eyes and looked at me, wetting his lips as he thrust harder.

Kieran moved around to Ethan's side and kissed him full-on, but Ethan again seemed hesitant, meeting Kieran's lips with half-hearted eagerness. He wasn't distracted this time, I was sure of it. It was hesitation.

But as quickly as he'd aroused my concern, Ethan alleviated it, his cheek hollowing as he deepened the kiss. One hand snaked around the back of Kieran's neck and Ethan's brow alternately tensed and relaxed as they made out and he fucked me.

A violent tremor pulled Ethan's lips away from Kieran's, and he closed his eyes, gasping for breath.

"Oh God," he whispered. When he opened his eyes, he met mine and wet his lips. Kissing Kieran one last time, he leaned down to kiss me. And there it was again, that tenderness, that hint of intimacy that was so incongruous to a situation like this. It wasn't just out of place in a hot, lust-driven threesome, it was out of place between us.

We aren't like this anymore, Ethan, my mind wanted to cry out. But my lips accepted—embraced—his kiss with equal gentleness. I returned his kiss like I wanted it this way because— *No. No. This isn't how it should be.*

Abruptly, Ethan broke the kiss and sat up. Before I could even reel from the kiss that shouldn't have been, Kieran took his place. He kissed me deeply and passionately as Ethan fucked me harder. My worries and concerns were lost in Kieran's desperate kiss and Ethan's incredible, perfect thrusts. As I combed my fingers through Kieran's hair, he kissed me, his tongue finding and toying with my piercing.

Still kissing Kieran, I looked up at Ethan. Our eyes met, but only for a moment. He closed his and looked away, taking in a sharp breath. Alarm once again raised the hairs on the back of my neck, but then he exhaled and threw his head back, driving himself into me just the way I wanted him to.

Relief swept over me. Whatever I thought I saw, it was only my imagination. Yet why did I keep imagining these things?

"Oh fuck..." Ethan exhaled hard. His rhythm faltered, his brow furrowed. "*Fuck.*"

Was that frustration?

No, I'm imagining things again. That's a man on the verge, no reason for concern.

But then he slowed down.

Slower still.

Stopped.

Even with the decrease in speed, his halt was abrupt and unexpected. He released another breath, and this time I knew it was a sound of something other than arousal. But what? Pain? Anger?

Kieran stopped and glanced at Ethan, then back at me.

"What's wrong?" I said.

Ethan's shoulders dropped. Closing his eyes, he exhaled hard, and the sound of frustration became one of surrender. Defeat.

Ice shot through my veins. "Ethan?"

"I can't do this." He pulled out slowly, taking in a breath through his teeth.

Kieran and I exchanged alarmed glances, then looked at Ethan.

"What's wrong?" Kieran asked. "Is—"

"I just can't do it." Ethan stood and picked up his clothes, then disappeared into the master bathroom. A moment later, the shower turned on.

I stared at the closed door, my mind reeling. Kieran pushed himself up. We didn't look at each other. Didn't speak. I closed my eyes and let out a breath that sounded a great deal like Ethan's frustrated, surrendered exhalation.

Feet padded quietly on the carpet beside the bed. Clothing rustled and the jingle of a belt buckle was quickly muffled.

Footsteps disappeared down the hall. Floorboards on the stairs creaked. A door closed.

In the master bathroom, the shower turned off, so I got up and grabbed my clothes.

Downstairs, Kieran was in the shower. I waited in my room until I was sure he was back in his, then went in to take a shower myself.

No matter how hot I turned the water, it wasn't enough to warm the cold, sick feeling in my gut. Letting water rush through my hair and down my neck and shoulders, I relived the threesome in my mind. Over and over, I watched us going through the motions and berated myself each time I came to one of those moments when I knew something was wrong, when I knew Ethan was hesitating. Though he'd quickly masked it every time, I knew. I'd taken arousal over instinct, pretended it wasn't happening, and now this.

"Fuck," I muttered to myself.

The water eventually turned cold, so I shut it off. As I dried myself and got ready for bed, I couldn't even look at myself in the mirror.

What had we done?

What had I done?

In bed, I lay in the darkness, staring at the ceiling. The house was dead silent for the rest of the night, but I wondered if anyone slept.

Chapter Thirty-one

Ethan didn't look up when I walked into the kitchen, but his posture stiffened enough that I knew he was aware of my presence. He poured his coffee and stepped away from the coffee pot so I could pour mine.

"Hey," I said.

He muttered something into his cup, but still didn't look in my direction. Instead, he busied himself making his lunch, cursing under his breath when his hands shook. When he paused to take a drink, I couldn't stand the silence anymore.

"Ethan, are you—"

He slammed his cup down so hard the sound echoed through the kitchen and coffee splashed onto his hand. "Fucking hell," he growled, jerking his hand back and turning to run cold water over it.

"You okay?" I asked.

"I'm fine." He grabbed a towel to dry his hand.

Swallowing hard, I said, "I didn't just mean your hand."

"Neither did I." He tossed the towel aside and put his coffee cup in the sink.

"What about last—"

"What about it?" he snapped, glaring at me. "It happened. Deal with it."

"Yeah, I realize it happened. I don't suppose you'll enlighten me as to why?"

He opened his mouth to speak, but footsteps turned both our heads. Kieran appeared in the doorway and stopped dead, eyes flicking back and forth between Ethan and me.

Ethan grabbed his briefcase and, with neither a word nor a look, he left.

Kieran and I didn't move or speak as the downstairs door opened and closed, then the garage door did the same. After a moment, Ethan's engine faded into the distance, leaving Kieran and me alone in uncomfortable silence. I'd hoped that Ethan's departure would reduce the awkwardness by at least a third, but the tension didn't diminish in the slightest.

Kieran glared at me. "So was it worth it?"

I blinked. "Kieran, I didn't—"

"Didn't know things would be awkward this time?" He snorted. "I should have known. It was last time. Why would this be any different?"

"Look, it's more complicated than I—"

"Yeah, I know," he snapped. "I fucking know, and that's why I never should have gotten involved. I'll give you props, though, Rhett, you really know how to persuade a guy to ignore his better judgment. Maybe if you'd tried the same technique with Ethan, he'd have stuck around a bit longer."

I set my jaw. "Kieran, I'm sorry, I didn't realize it would be like this. It was awkward last time, I know, but I thought Ethan and I had things sorted out. I don't have a clue what happened last night."

"Well, good luck getting it sorted. Just do me a favor and leave me the fuck out of it."

"Hey, we never brought you into this to—"

"Yeah, but you *did* bring me into it. You brought me into it when you decided to try it again knowing full well it didn't work last time, so, big shock when it was even worse this time." He shook his head and swore under his breath. "I don't know what the fuck is going on between the two of you, if you're just in goddamned denial—"

"Denial?" I eyed him. "What are you talking about?"

"Oh, please." He rolled his eyes and started to leave. "You two act like you don't want each other, even though it's so painfully obvious to anyone else that you do."

That hit me in the chest. "Kieran, that's ridiculous." The words came out as little more than a feeble whisper.

"Is it?" One foot out the door, he looked at me over his shoulder. "So I'm just imagining all of it?"

"Ethan and I are done." My voice shook, but not with the anger I tried to inject into it. "Whatever it is you think you're seeing—"

He threw his head back and laughed. "Listen to yourself, Rhett. You don't even believe what you're saying."

I gritted my teeth. "Kieran, what—"

"I have never seen two people so hellbent on pretending they can't stand each other. Any *idiot* can see that you guys are anything but over each other." His expression darkened even more and his lip curled into a snarl as he added, "I just happened to be the idiot that got roped into helping you figure it out. You're on your own now."

"Do you really think he would have walked out last night if that was the case?" I called after him as he again started to leave.

He paused in the doorway. "I don't know. I really don't. But I know what I've seen and I know what I saw last night. Fuck if

I know if you two will ever figure it out or what you'll do and, quite frankly, I don't give a shit." He turned to face me, stabbing the air with one finger. "All I know is that I don't appreciate being the pawn you play against each other, so—" He paused, dropping his gaze, and for the first time, his angry exterior cracked. When he looked at me again, the pain in his eyes turned my blood to ice and my knees to water. His voice was unsteady when he said, "Find someone else to use while you figure it out."

Without another word, he stormed out of the kitchen, leaving me with the echoes of his words and footsteps.

My knees tried to give out, so I grabbed the counter for support. Guilt twisted and churned in my stomach.

No matter how much I tried to deny or rationalize, Kieran was absolutely right. On all counts. We'd used him. No, *I* had used him. I'd convinced myself it was just some casual sex and a little harmless fun, but I knew from the start what I was doing. I had used him to try to convince myself I could use Ethan. I was too damned stubborn to admit I still wanted Ethan and, in the process of lying to myself, I'd managed to hurt Kieran.

And what had come of all of this besides angry, uncomfortable silence? Nothing but the cold realization that I had hurt both of them and I still wanted Ethan.

Everything I'd done to convince myself I wanted Ethan gone had only driven home the point that I wanted him to stay.

"Fuck," I whispered into the stillness. "What have I done?"

Chapter Thirty-two

It was an unseasonably cold evening, but at least it was warmer out on the balcony than in the house. Kieran and Ethan were home. No one was speaking. Maybe they spoke to each other, but I doubted it. Not with the eerie silence that chilled every room in the house for the last few days and nights. There was no interaction at all besides passing in the halls. We all carefully avoided each other in common areas of the house, retreating to bedrooms whenever we could. When occupying the same space couldn't be avoided, there were cold shoulders all around. There hadn't been this much tension under our roof since before Ethan and I broke up.

Something had to give eventually. I was fairly sure the only way this was going to break was when one—or better yet, both—moved out.

When the sliding glass door opened, I cringed. The hairs on the back of my neck stood on end, my senses seeking to identify the newcomer even though I couldn't bring myself to turn around and look. I wasn't quite sure who I hoped it would be, who was the lesser of two evils.

The door slid closed, and a scuff of a shoe on concrete gave me the feeling of being locked in a lion's den. The balcony was small to begin with, but now it was downright claustrophobic.

I held my breath, wondering who. And why.

A hand on my shoulder startled the hell out of me, and I spun around, narrowly missing Ethan's chest with my elbow.

"Whoa, easy." He put up his hands. He was backlit, his face hidden in shadow. "Sorry, didn't mean to startle you."

"Don't worry about it." I gripped the railing for balance. Anger and confusion twisted in my chest. Was he still so obtuse that he thought I'd want him to touch me when he'd barely said two words to me in days?

Except I did want him to touch me, and for that, I hated myself.

Turning back to look out at the city, I rested my forearms on the railing and dug my piercing into the roof of my mouth.

"Mind if I stay out here?" His calm demeanor and the lack of hostility in his voice were strange after the way we'd last interacted. Alien. Incongruous. Even more jarring than his unexpected touch.

"No, sure," I murmured. "Plenty of room."

He stood beside the railing, but didn't touch it. For a long moment, neither of us spoke. I had a feeling something was on his mind, so I left it to him to break the silence.

"Kieran's leaving," he said finally.

"I figured he had to work tonight."

"No, I mean he's leaving. He's gone to work, yes, but I mean he's moving out. At the end of the month."

My shoulders dropped slightly, caving under the weight of both relief and disappointment. Looking at him, I said, "You let him out of the lease?"

He nodded. "I would have asked you first, but, given the circumstances, I couldn't see arguing with him about it."

"So he's still upset?"

"Can you blame him?"

"No, definitely not." Silence descended between us again.

After a moment, Ethan said, "We really fucked up with him."

"Yeah, I know." I sighed. "It was hot, but..." I shook my head. "I guess we should have known it was a bad idea. All of it."

"You'd think we would have learned the first time. The second time? Christ, what were we thinking?"

"No idea." My shoulder tingled where he'd touched me, and I couldn't help but wonder what *he* was thinking when he walked out on the balcony and put his hand on me. Especially after everything that had happened recently. I wasn't sure I wanted to know, just as I wasn't sure I wanted him to know the conclusions I'd come to after my argument with Kieran.

So I didn't ask. Shifting my gaze from Ethan back to the glittering skyline, I said, "So what do we do now? Get another roommate?"

"Probably the best thing to do. As long as neither of us fucks him this time."

I thought about suggesting a female roommate. At least there would be no concerns about *both* of us ending up in bed with her, but I kept it to myself. The thought of another roommate was an unnerving unknown, a potential for more conflict between us that we just didn't need.

I absently ran my tongue stud along the backs of my teeth. Kieran's departure would help ease some of the tension in the house, but I hated that we'd driven him out and driven a bigger wedge between Ethan and me.

"For the moment," Ethan said, breaking the silence. "I guess it's just us."

A shiver ran down my spine. "Yeah, I guess it is."

"Maybe before someone else moves in, it might behoove us to try to get back on civil terms."

I shrugged. "We're being civil now, aren't we?"

"Yeah, but for how long?"

I didn't have an answer.

When his hand made contact again, my shoulder jerked away as if I'd been shocked. Staring at him, I gritted my teeth, biting back anger at his sheer nerve.

"What the fuck was that?" I said.

He laughed bitterly. "I guess I shouldn't be surprised by that."

"What? That I don't—"

"You know, I was actually starting to get used to you letting me touch you again." The sudden fury in his voice startled me more than the physical contact had. "I should have known better than to take that for granted."

"What's that supposed to mean? You're the one who walked out the other night, and now—"

"Yes, I did. And I had my reasons."

"Which I fucking *tried* to ask you about, but, ever so conveniently, you walked out again. Now you're pissed at me for pulling away when you touch me?"

He let out a sharp breath. "Look, the other night was a mistake. It just..." He trailed off, making a frustrated gesture. "It just was."

"Yeah, we've established that." I pushed myself off the railing and stood upright. "It was a fucking mistake. Now you want to tell me why I'm suddenly to blame for having the audacity to not want you touching me tonight?"

"It's not just tonight."

"Oh, really?" I folded my arms across my chest. "Then when exactly are we talking about?"

"Come on, Rhett. The last two or three years, it was a gamble if you'd pull away from me. I guess I've been spoiled the last few weeks because, for once, you didn't act like I repulsed you, so I hoped tonight..." He trailed off and shrugged.

I blinked. "What are you talking about?"

"You don't remember?" he said. I couldn't tell if he sounded angry, hurt, bitter. "All the times I wanted you and you shrugged me off?"

"You mean all the times we could barely look at each other and you wanted to fuck anyway?" I clenched my teeth. "Like tonight? Sorry, Ethan, I get as horny as the next man, but I've never needed to get my rocks off quite so—"

"Is *that* what you think I was doing?" Though his face was hidden in shadow, I could just make out the outline of his eyebrows as they jumped. "Just using you as a substitute for my hand?"

"Well, when you wouldn't speak to me, but you were perfectly willing to fuck me," I said, shrugging, "what was I supposed to think?"

"Jesus Christ, Rhett." He shook his head and slouched over the railing. "I wasn't thinking 'oh hell, we're not speaking, but maybe he'll let me get my damned rocks off anyway'."

"Then what *were* you thinking?"

"How much I liked being turned away, apparently," he muttered.

"So I'm supposed to feel guilty for turning you away when you—"

He jerked upright and stared at me. "I don't suppose it ever occurred to you that I was, oh, I don't know, reaching out to you, did it?"

My mouth went dry. "What?"

He looked at me. "Every time, every fucking time," he said, the angry growl nearly masking the unsteadiness in his voice. "I was thinking that I wanted you. Not just a quick fuck and an orgasm, *you.*" He took a breath and dropped his gaze. "And when things were going south, I thought maybe if we still had something in the bedroom, then we still had something worth saving outside of it."

I stared at him, completely at a loss for words.

He turned and leaned on the railing again, staring out at the city and furrowing his brow as if the view required intense concentration. "I thought if we could still have sex, then maybe we were still on the same page. And we could talk later. The way we did after the first threesome."

"Like makeup sex before we'd made up?"

He rubbed the back of his neck, still avoiding my eyes. "You know, they don't call it 'making love' for nothing."

The air in my lungs refused to move for a moment. I could neither breathe in nor out, but finally managed to whisper, "Why didn't you tell me, Ethan?"

"I was trying to." His voice sounded like it was on the verge of cracking. "I was trying to tell you in the only way I could think to get through to you." He paused, drawing a breath. "I didn't know how else to say it."

Running a shaking hand through my hair, I pressed my tongue stud against the roof of my mouth.

He took a breath. "Why do you think we always got along better when we were having sex all the time?"

Clearing my throat, I looked at him. "I always thought we were having sex all the time because we were getting along."

"Maybe we were." He dropped his gaze, focusing on something below the balcony. "Or maybe when we were on the same page in bed, we were closer to the same page everywhere else."

I couldn't argue with him. As the last ten years flashed through my mind, he was right. And over the last two or three years, the more we'd argued, the less we'd had sex. I'd stopped initiating it at all. Before long, we didn't even bother with makeup sex anymore. Cringing, I thought of all the times I'd pulled away from his touch until he eventually just stopped reaching for me at all. From there, the slow, steady downward spiral picked up speed and before I knew it, it was over. I'd been so angry when he said he wanted to end our relationship, not realizing that he'd simply been agreeing with a decision I'd made months before.

"Jesus," I breathed. I looked out at the city, blinking rapidly when the distant lights tried to blur.

"That's why I started this whole thing, Rhett. When I came on to you that night in the kitchen." He swallowed. "I couldn't stand living here when you couldn't stand me. I hoped that if you didn't, you know, if you didn't turn me away that night, maybe there was some chance..."

I wet my lips, gripping the railing to keep my hands steady. "What about Kieran?"

"What about him?"

"You didn't wait long before you got involved with him." I tried to keep the bitterness out of my tone. "Were you just trying to get back at me? Or make me jealous?"

He turned and looked me in the eye. "I was trying to get over you. He was attractive, he was available..." Ethan shrugged. "And I'm not going to lie, when I found out about you two—" He paused, avoiding my eyes. "I'm not going to lie, I was jealous."

"Jealous? Why the hell—"

"Yes, I was, okay? Pardon me for getting jealous," he snapped. "I'm human, Rhett."

"What business did you have getting jealous? You had him first. What? Just didn't like sharing him?"

He turned toward me and even in the low light, the intensity in his eyes nearly knocked me back a step. "I was never once jealous of you with Kieran."

"Bullshit, you weren't. You just said—"

"I was jealous of *him*."

"You—" I caught myself.

He took a deep breath and closed his eyes as he leaned against the railing, his shoulders slumping slightly. After a moment, he looked up and swallowed hard. "I was jealous because he had you."

All I could do was stare at him.

He moistened his lips. "I know I shouldn't have been. But I was. I was, and I am."

"But you've..." I shook my head. "You've had me, right along with him. There was nothing to be jealous of."

"Maybe not. All I know is that it killed me to see the two of you together. So that's why I came on to you, and why I joined in that night. I thought maybe if we were all together, if you were sleeping with him and with me, that maybe it would take the edge off the jealousy. Maybe..." He trailed off. Sniffing sharply, he exhaled hard and looked at the city.

I followed his gaze. Seattle was certainly under some scrutiny tonight. I wondered what I had stopped noticing first— our view of the Space Needle or Ethan.

"Why didn't you tell me?" I whispered.

"I spent the last two years trying to tell you, Rhett," he said. "In every way I could think of short of just coming out and saying it—"

"Why not just come out and say it?"

He turned to me slowly, swallowing hard, and his voice shook as he whispered, "Because I was afraid of what I'd hear."

I couldn't speak. Every word cut deeper than the last, especially with the unsteadiness in his voice. How could I have been so blind? I'd had no idea Ethan hurt this badly.

But he wasn't finished.

"The other night, when I walked out," he said, focusing intently on something in the distance. "I realized I couldn't handle being nothing more than a fuck buddy to you. Not when I know what it's like—" He paused, clearing his throat. "What it's like to be more than that. And I walked out because I realized just how..." He closed his eyes, and his cheek rippled as he set his jaw.

Fear of the answer nearly caught the question in my throat, but I managed to whisper, "You realized what?"

He took a deep breath. "I realized how much of a mistake it was to leave you, and just how far out of my reach you are now."

"Jesus, Ethan," I said. "The whole time, over the last few years, I thought you were pulling away from me."

"I only pulled away from you because it hurt too much to watch you push me away," he said. "I thought if I just stepped away completely, ripped the bandage off instead of pulling it slowly, then it would..." He paused, taking a deep breath. "That it would hurt like hell for a while, but it would be over and I could get over it."

"That's why you're moving to Toronto, isn't it?"

"Yes. If we hadn't been stuck with the house, I'd have been long gone. As far from here as I could get."

I swallowed. "As far from me as you could get?"

He closed his eyes, exhaled slowly and nodded.

I flinched. That admission stung, and not because he wanted to get so far away from me. It hurt because I'd driven him so far away. All this time, I'd resented him for pulling away, never realizing that I had done more than my fair share of pushing him away.

"Ethan, if you'd told me..." I exhaled, trying to keep my composure.

His voice cracked almost imperceptibly when he said, "Would you have listened?"

What could I say? He was right. He knew it, I knew it; there was no point in denying it.

Taking a deep breath, pushing aside all the fears that tried to come to the surface, I put my hand over his on the railing. His gaze darted to where we made contact, and I silently pleaded with him not to pull away. He didn't and, a second later, his eyes rose to meet mine.

I squeezed his hand gently. "I'm listening now."

He swallowed hard and looked at my hand again. *Please don't tell me it's too little too late.* The hand beneath mine loosened its grip on the railing. *Please don't pull away from me.* Slowly, he freed his hand, and something cold and heavy sank in my chest. *Please don't.* Our eyes met, his expression unreadable.

Please...

I held my breath as he turned toward me. As he raised his hand slowly. Though my eyes never left his, I sensed his hand coming closer to my face. When he touched me, his skin was still cool from the railing, but that wasn't what made me shiver.

The distance between us was just a few inches of evening air, but his arm seemed to bridge a span of miles and his featherlight touch crumbled walls that had taken years to build. His fingers moved into my hair, and his other arm slid around my waist. My hands wanted to go to him, but in disbelief, I couldn't move.

He took a breath and, for a moment, I thought he was about to speak. Instead, he drew me to him and kissed me.

It was a gentle kiss, just his lips against mine as we breathed each other in, but it eased a deep, consuming sense of loss I hadn't even been fully aware of. I wrapped my arms around him, holding him closer and letting him overwhelm my senses. For all that had been said and all we'd been through, it was this kiss—this deliberate, silent return to the way things should have been—that allowed me to release my breath for the first time in months. In *years*.

I had to break the kiss just to look at him, to remind myself that this was real. Our eyes met, and it was. He was here. My world was back on its axis.

There were a thousand things I wanted to say, to ask, to know, but words hadn't done us a lot of good. All they'd done was keep me from hearing everything he'd tried to tell me all along. Talking could wait until we'd said all the things we needed to say.

So I kissed him again.

Chapter Thirty-three

Ethan's hand cradled the back of my neck as we sank slowly onto my bed. His skin was hot against mine, and his kiss was warm and tender. Nothing divided us anymore. Nothing remained between us. And still, I couldn't get close enough to him. The smell of his skin, the taste of his kiss, the heat of his body, it was all too much and not nearly enough.

Everything happened in slow motion. We moved and touched with a kind of tenderness I didn't think we were capable of anymore, actually taking the time to feel and taste each other, memorizing territory we'd once taken for granted until we'd forgotten.

We only stopped long enough to get a condom and lube out of the drawer, and once those were taken care of, we were right back in each other's arms. He rolled me onto my back and took me inside him, our bodies moving slowly, smoothly, fluidly. All the while, his eyes were locked on mine and mine on his.

Everything about this was hot. Intimate. *Honest.* For the first time in a long time, it was uncomplicated. It should have been simple when it was just sex, but now it was simple because it was *right.* I just couldn't believe it was real. I touched his face, seeking tactile confirmation of what my eyes just couldn't comprehend. He turned and kissed my palm, closing his eyes and releasing a warm, uneven breath against my skin.

So many times we couldn't stand the sight of each other, but now I couldn't look anywhere but right at him. Every time we touched, I couldn't believe we'd ever thrown this away. I was inside him, but he was under my skin.

Meeting my eyes again, he leaned down and kissed me. His kiss made me dizzy, but not because of his incredibly talented mouth this time. It was, in every sense of the word, overwhelming. Not just being this close to him, but realizing how far away he'd been. Realizing how much ground we'd lost and regained. Maybe we had to go through all of that so we could be here now. We had to walk away to understand why we had to come back. We had to break to mend.

A shudder straightened his spine, and he pushed himself up on his arms, closing his eyes and throwing his head back. I reached between us and stroked him, letting every display of arousal—his brow furrowing, his lips parting with a sudden breath, the cords standing out on his neck—hypnotize me. My hand moved faster with every gasp of breath he took, until he arched his back and moaned. A violent shudder shook him so hard it took *my* breath away, and it was all I could do to hold back when he came with a throaty roar.

When his orgasm subsided with a heavy sigh, Ethan's spine seemed to crumble, starting at the small of his back and slowly collapsing one vertebra at a time. When his trembling arms and shoulders couldn't hold him up, I put my arms around him and pulled him down into a deep, breathless kiss.

After he'd caught his breath, he rose off me slowly, and I reached for the tissues and lube. He lay on his back beside me and, after I'd put on some more lube, I joined him. I sat up, running my hand down his thigh as I guided my cock to him. Pushing into him slowly, I took a few slow, easy strokes, then continued with that gentle cadence as I leaned down to kiss him.

As I picked up speed, I lifted myself on my arms for leverage, but still I couldn't take my eyes off him.

Neither of us spoke at all. We were usually so vocal—begging, demanding, whispering, moaning—but we were nearly silent now. Just moving. Breathing. Touching. *Seeing* each other and saying so, so much. All those times he'd tried to tell me with a touch what he couldn't put into words, when I'd been too wrapped up in the icy silence to hear him, I understood now. As we spoke in this raw, unadorned language, I realized how much I stood to lose and how much I'd very nearly lost.

He raised his head off the pillow and kissed me, cupping the back of my neck with one hand and caressing my face with the other. His hips moved with mine, pulling me deeper and coaxing my body into a faster, hungrier rhythm.

As I moved faster, we couldn't breathe let alone kiss, so I just let my head fall beside his. Sweat and aftershave—that familiar, heady aftershave that simply smelled like Ethan—mesmerized my senses along with the scuff of his five o'clock shadow against my jaw.

A helpless moan escaped my throat, and I closed my eyes as electricity surged through every nerve ending in my body. I gritted my teeth to keep my orgasm back for just a few more seconds, but when Ethan trailed his fingertips up my back, I let go. With a choked cry, I thrust deep inside him and came so hard my eyes welled up.

Sinking against him, I rested my forehead on his shoulder as he ran his fingers through my sweaty hair. I slid my arms under his back and just held on, just breathed him in and let this moment be.

Eventually, I pushed myself up on one trembling arm and touched his face with my other hand. He lifted his head and kissed me, first lightly, then deeply. When he settled back onto the pillow, we just looked at each other.

Only our breathing interrupted the silence now. That and the occasional gentle brush of fingers through hair or skin across stubble. It seemed like a lifetime since the last words had passed between us in the form of my whispered "I'm listening now" on the balcony.

Ethan watched his fingertips trail down the side of my face and, when his eyes again met mine, he broke the silence:

"I never stopped loving you."

I smiled and kissed him again, then whispered, "I never stopped loving you, either." I thought I had. There were times I thought I hated him.

Never in my life had I been so glad to be wrong.

Chapter Thirty-four

I rested my head on Ethan's shoulder and watched his fingers lace between mine on his chest. It must have been years since we'd been this close, this intimate.

The air between us was unsettled, though, the silence heavy with something that didn't want to remain unsaid.

I shifted onto my side and looked at him, but he didn't look back at me, nor did he speak.

"What's on your mind?" I asked.

Still avoiding my eyes, he watched his fingers trail up and down my arm. "I actually came out on the balcony to talk to you." Twin lines formed between his eyebrows. "Not just about Kieran."

Something cold settled in my chest. "What about?"

He bit his lip, watching his fingers again. "They offered me the job," he said, almost sighing. "The one in Toronto."

My heart sank, but I finally managed a noncommittal "Oh."

"They offered me a lot more than I expected. More money. A lot more opportunity to move up."

"You deserve it," I said, barely breathing at all. "You've worked hard." The silence that fell was even heavier than before and lingered for an uncomfortably long moment until he spoke again.

"Look at me." He touched my face, brushing his thumb across my cheekbone, but I couldn't meet his eyes. We'd finally landed back on common ground and, before I'd even had a chance to find my equilibrium, the world had shifted again.

"Rhett, look at me," he said again, softer this time. "Please." When I did, he swallowed hard. "Do you want me to stay?"

My lips parted and I blinked. "Ethan, you've got a hell of an opportunity, you can't—"

"I am. Tell me you want me to stay and I'll call them and turn down the offer."

I dropped my gaze again. "I can't ask you to give up something like that."

"And you're not. This is my choice. They're waiting on my decision, but before I make it, I have to know if..." He trailed off, pursing his lips.

"If?"

He took a breath and looked me in the eye. "If there's a reason for me to stay."

I wet my lips. "You have to ask?"

"I want to know." He swallowed again. "I want to hear you say it."

I put my hand over his, and my voice threatened to crack when I spoke. "Yes," I whispered. "I want you to stay." The sound of those words rolling off my tongue almost moved me to tears. With all the things we hadn't said, and all the things I'd tried to convince myself I did and didn't feel, that was the simple, raw truth and had been since the beginning. Clearing my throat, I took a breath. "I don't want you to leave."

"Then I won't." He lifted his head and crossed the narrow space between us, kissing me gently. The next kiss lingered. Deepened. I wrapped my arms around him, and he rolled on top of me, every breath and touch echoing my desire for him to stay and his promise not to go.

He broke the kiss and smiled at me, but the smile faltered a little. Touching my face, he said, "We've been through a lot. It's not going to be perfect overnight."

I nodded, trailing my fingers down the back of his neck. "I know."

"But I'm willing to work at it if you are."

"I am." I couldn't imagine not working at it now. Not now that I knew just how much I had to lose. Just how much I'd almost lost. Running my fingers through his hair, I said, "I definitely am."

He kissed me again. "I think we owe Kieran for this."

"No kidding. Assuming he'll speak to us."

Ethan shrugged. "We can talk to him. Tell him we fucked up." Then a devilish grin spread across his lips. "And assuming he'll listen to us, I think I know how we can repay him."

Chapter Thirty-five

Kieran worked until closing on Saturday night, so he slept until almost noon on Sunday. When he finally emerged, showered and dressed, Ethan and I were in the living room drinking coffee.

He walked past us, eyes focused straight ahead and lips pressed together in a thin, bleached line as he disappeared into the kitchen.

Ethan and I exchanged looks and silent nods. Then we stood and followed him. When he saw us, Kieran's spine straightened and he set his jaw. If ever I'd seen him looking both uncomfortable and irritated, it was now.

"Got a few minutes?" Ethan asked.

Kieran popped the tab on a soda and shrugged. "I have all damned day." The sarcastic edge to his voice told me he had no intention of giving *us* all damned day.

Ethan and I glanced at each other. Then he said, "We just want to talk. About...everything."

Kieran's lips tightened, but he made a "go on" gesture with his soda can.

Ethan shifted his weight. "Listen, we never should have put you between us." He paused. "Literally or figuratively."

Kieran allowed the briefest hint of amusement to pull up

the corner of his mouth, but it was gone as quickly as it had come.

"You were right," I said. "Everything you said to me the other night. And I'm sorry."

"As am I," Ethan said.

He eyed both of us, then nodded. "Okay, I can accept that."

Another look passed between Ethan and me before he continued. "There's, um, there's a bit more."

Kieran's eyebrows jumped. "Oh, really?" Ethan's arm snaked around my waist, and Kieran set his jaw and looked away, the soda can crinkling in his fist.

Ethan took a breath and spoke gently. "We're back together—"

"Congrats," Kieran said through clenched teeth.

"It never would have happened without you, Kieran," I said. "And honestly, we can't thank you enough."

"Oh, really?" Kieran growled. "Gee, I'm touched."

"Look, Kieran, the last threesome." I paused. "It was a mistake."

He laughed bitterly. "Yeah, that would be an understatement."

"I mean it was a mistake because it happened for all the wrong reasons," I said.

"Are you saying there are any right reasons for something like that to happen?" He rolled his eyes and slammed the can down on the counter. "I mean, *besides* three people who just wanted to fuck each other and not try to use sex to manipulate each other?"

"That's exactly why it should have happened, and why it did the first time," Ethan said.

"And it's exactly why we want to do it again," I said.

Kieran released a cough of laughter. "You can't be serious."

"We are," Ethan said. "All the bullshit was between Rhett and me. It had nothing to do with you, and we never should have dragged you into the middle of it."

"Yeah, yeah, yeah, I've heard this crap before." Kieran rolled his eyes. "It's all settled, it's all resolved, you guys are cool now, it has—"

"Kieran," Ethan said. "We want to do this because we fucked up the last two times and we want to make it up to you."

"By starting it all over again?" Kieran drummed his fingers on the counter. "Are you crazy?"

"Look," I said. "The one thing I think we can all agree on was that the sex was hot. The threesomes were hot."

Kieran snorted. "Yeah, right up until—"

"Until I walked out." Ethan exhaled and looked away. He took a breath. "Which I did because there were things I needed to say to him." He gestured toward me. "And all of that's been said."

Kieran pursed his lips, but didn't speak.

"Listen, I don't think any of us can argue that it was hot," I said. "And we want it again *without* the bullshit this time. Without all the drama."

"We're serious," Ethan said. "If you don't want to do it, we won't twist your arm. But we want it. You're leaving here in a few weeks, and we want you to leave on a positive note. Not like this."

"This has nothing to do with trying to fuck with each other's minds, or playing games. None of that," I said. "This time, it's just sex. Just like it should have been every time."

"So you two are back together, but you still want me in

your bed with you?" Kieran scowled. "I wouldn't think you'd want anyone between you again."

"Having you between us brought us back together," I said. "I know it sounds crazy, but everything about this, from the day you moved in, has been crazy."

"I'll give you that." Kieran laughed softly. His eyes flicked back and forth between us. For a long moment, he chewed his lip and alternately looked at either of us and the expanse of tile floor between us. Finally he let out a breath and shrugged. "Well, as long as it's just sex, and you guys are damn sure that all the other bullshit is settled between you, then who am I to argue?"

Ethan and I exchanged mischievous grins and we both started toward him. Then Ethan said, "There is one more little difference this time."

Kieran's eyebrows jumped. "Oh?"

"Yeah." I kissed the side of Kieran's neck. "This time, it's all about you."

Chapter Thirty-six

Following them into Ethan's bedroom was eerily like returning to the scene of the crime. So much had changed, and yet we were the same men in the same place. The hairs on the back of my neck stood on end. Had everything changed enough, or was this another mistake?

Kieran hesitated briefly before stepping through the door, just long enough to make me wonder if he was going to continue or call things off before they started. But continue he did.

Ethan put his hands on Kieran's waist and leaned in to kiss his neck. Speaking so softly I could barely hear him, he said, "Are you sure you're okay with this?"

Kieran's gaze darted toward me, then he lowered his chin and kissed Ethan. Everything about his kiss answered Ethan's question in no uncertain terms, especially Ethan's startled half-step back before he recovered and came back for more.

I stood behind Kieran and slid my hands under his shirt. Running my palms up his back, I brought his shirt up with it. Ethan and I pushed Kieran's shirt over his head and out of the way. Kieran shivered when I kissed between his shoulder blades.

Metal jingled, and Kieran drew a sharp breath. With the insistent rustle of fabric and scratch of a zipper, he tensed even more, and when he groaned, I knew Ethan's hand had found its mark.

I stood back and watched them, watched Ethan nearly drive Kieran to his trembling knees with both his touch and that incredible kiss. I couldn't help but lick my lips in search of a lingering taste of his mouth. As if on cue, Ethan broke the kiss and licked his own lips as he looked at Kieran.

"Tell us what you want," he said. "This is all about you."

Kieran didn't answer immediately, but his cheek rose slowly, and when he looked over his shoulder at me, I wasn't at all surprised to see a grin on his face. He reached back and grabbed my shirt, pulling me toward him. As he kissed me, another buckle jingled and Ethan exhaled hard. Kieran's kiss made me dizzy. I couldn't decide if I tasted him or Ethan or both, but my head spun nonetheless.

"I think you both know what I want," he said as he went for my belt.

"But this is—" The words stopped in my throat when his fingers traced the outline of my cock through my jeans. Closing my eyes, I swallowed, trying to find my voice again. "This is about *you.*"

"I know," he said, drawing my zipper down. "And this is what I want." Another buckle clanged, and Ethan released a sharp breath.

"Jesus," Ethan whispered. "I have never known a man who likes sucking cock like you do."

Kieran just smiled and knelt in front of us. Ethan and I both exhaled, then he moaned softly. A second later, Kieran ran his tongue along the length of my cock, and I shuddered.

Desperate to do something with my mouth, I pulled Ethan into a kiss. We got rid of our shirts, desperate to be close to each other's hot, bare skin. We kissed and touched and alternately gasped and shuddered as Kieran stroked and sucked our cocks. He devoured mine—and presumably Ethan's, judging by his shivers and moans—as hungrily as Ethan and I kissed each other.

Ethan broke the kiss, furrowing his brow and taking short, shallow gasps of breath. "Oh fuck, don't stop..."

I held one side of his neck and kissed the other, his voice vibrating and pulse quickening against my lips and tongue. "You're so fucking hot when you're this close," I whispered, flicking my tongue behind his ear. He shivered and gripped my shoulders tighter, his body swaying slightly as balance gave way to impending release.

"Oh my God..." he groaned. I put a hand on his hip to steady him, and he held my shoulders as his body trembled more and more with each gasp.

"Jesus, Kieran," I said, kissing the underside of Ethan's jaw. "Do you realize what you're doing to him?" I laughed softly as a tremor rippled through Ethan. "You're going to drive him out of his goddamned mind if you keep doing that."

A whimper of surrender escaped Ethan's lips, and a downward glance confirmed that Kieran had doubled his efforts as I egged him on. In a low growl, I said, "Don't stop, Kieran, I fucking love what you're doing to him."

Ethan's breath caught. "Oh...fuck...oh...*fuck*..."

I nipped his earlobe and whispered, "Don't hold back. Let him taste how much he turns you on."

As soon as the words were out, Ethan's knees buckled, and he held onto me for dear life as he came with a moan that was barely more than a sigh.

As Kieran released him and stood, Ethan's balance wavered again, so I guided him back against the bed. Kieran grabbed the back of my neck and pulled me into a deep, hungry kiss that was heady with Ethan's semen. I held his face in both hands, losing myself in his kiss. His hands slid down my sides and he pulled me closer so his hard cock pressed against my hip.

"Now *that* is hot," Ethan said. I glanced at him, the memory of the last time flickering through my mind, but there was no apprehension in his eyes this time. No jealousy, no hesitation, just pure, mouthwatering lust.

He pushed himself away from the bed, faltering only for a second, and put his hands on Kieran's shoulders. "Don't stop on account of me," he whispered, bending to kiss between Kieran's shoulder blades.

Kieran's spine straightened and he let out a ragged breath just before I kissed him again. I stroked his cock, my own aching with need every time his twitched in my hand or his breath cooled my skin. I wanted him. I wanted them. I'd never been so damned turned on in my life, and without all the tension and imbalance between us, none of us held back. Kisses were hungrier, touches more earnest, need less resistible.

Kieran suddenly broke away, panting unevenly against my lips, holding himself upright with a hand on my shoulder and the other on the back of my neck.

"Condom," he said breathlessly. "I need..." He closed his eyes and licked his lips. Ethan put his arms around Kieran's waist, steadying him even as he continued kissing the side of his neck. Kieran finally managed to murmur, "Need a condom."

Certain that Ethan would keep Kieran on his feet, I stepped away to get a condom.

"Who do you want first?" Ethan said to Kieran.

"You." Kieran nodded toward the bed. "On your back."

Ethan and I exchanged grins as Kieran took the condom. As Kieran put on the condom and some lube, Ethan did as he'd asked, lying on his back at the edge of the bed.

I had to bite my lip as I watched Kieran's hips move forward slightly before retreating, then advancing a little more. Ethan's back arched, and the bedcovers bunched in his clawing fingers.

I couldn't wait. I grabbed a condom, and Kieran shot me a startled look as I tore the wrapper. He exhaled through what sounded like chattering teeth and shivered.

I put my hands on his hips, and he slowed his thrusts, nearly stopping but not quite. When I pressed my cock against him, my hips mirroring his motions, he moaned and let his head fall forward.

"Told you this was all about you." Ethan pushed himself up to kiss Kieran. I knew the instant their lips met because a shudder ran up Kieran's spine, leaving goose bumps in its wake.

As Ethan rested back on the bed, I slid just the head of my cock into Kieran, pushing in, then pulling back, then pushing in again. He tried to lean back against me, trying to pull me deeper, but I kept control with my hands on his hips. Then, pressing my palms into his hips, I urged him forward, then drew him back with my fingertips, then guided him forward again, coaxing him back into a faster rhythm.

He got the message and fell into my smooth, easy tempo, withdrawing slowly from Ethan before pushing in once again. As he slid deeper into Ethan, I slid deeper into him, and his entire body quivered against mine as he simultaneously gave and took everything he could.

Over Kieran's shoulder, I met Ethan's eyes and he ran his tongue across his lower lip. When I thrust harder into Kieran, he moaned and in turn slammed into Ethan, who gasped and closed his eyes.

Our collective rhythm increased with every thrust, as did their moans and my own. Every tremor that ran through Kieran subsequently ran through me, and I wasn't going to last much longer, not like this, not when he felt so amazing and he and Ethan were both losing their goddamned minds.

"Oh God..." Someone groaned.

"Fuck, that's incredible..."

"Keep...doing...that..."

It was impossible to tell whose voice was whose. Even my own voice seemed to have a mind of its own and whatever I whispered or moaned or cursed tangled in the air, indistinguishable from anything Kieran or Ethan said.

"Oh...fuck...I'm—" A deep, helpless groan. "I'm gonna come, oh God..."

Whether or not the words came from my mouth, they echoed exactly what went through my mind. I clenched my teeth, trying to hold back even as I gave him—them—all I had.

Kieran threw his head back and his spine arched, causing both of us to falter for just a split second.

"Oh fuck," he moaned. "Fuck, I can't..." With a shudder, he thrust all the way into Ethan. I held his hips tighter and fucked him as he trembled and begged for more, more, more.

He slumped forward, and Ethan's hands appeared on the back of his neck. Ethan rose off the bed enough to kiss Kieran, and when he looked at me over Kieran's shoulder, eyes smoldering with insatiable lust, I couldn't hold back anymore.

They both grunted as I slammed into Kieran and came and, for a moment, in my delirious, intoxicated, completely overwhelmed state, I swore I was coming inside both of them.

I rested my forehead on Kieran's shoulder, trying not to put my full weight on both of them, as the last aftershocks surged through me. When I was sure I could move without passing out, I pulled out slowly and took care of the condom. Kieran pushed himself up, closing his eyes and exhaling as he did the same. Then we collapsed onto the bed on either side of Ethan.

For the longest time, we were all quiet, but the silence was comfortable. No uncertainty, no jealousy, no hostility. Kieran rested his head on Ethan's shoulder. I laced my fingers between Ethan's. His thumb ran back and forth along my hand, and we all just tried to catch our breath.

It was Kieran who finally broke the silence.

"I have to hand it to you guys." He shifted onto his stomach and propped himself up on his elbows. "This is probably one of the most unorthodox solutions to one of the most unorthodox situations I've ever heard of."

Ethan laughed. "Everything about this has been unorthodox from the beginning."

"We were just trying to be consistent." I grinned and rolled onto my side, still gently grasping Ethan's hand.

Kieran grinned. "Well, it worked, I'll give you that." His smile fell, but he didn't look unhappy. Serious, if anything. Concentrating, perhaps. "So you guys are really back together?"

Ethan glanced at me, smiling and squeezing my hand before looking back at Kieran. "Yeah, we are."

Kieran smiled and shook his head. "Only the two of you could reconcile over sex with someone else."

"Yeah, it's strange, but..." I shrugged. "The end justified the means."

"I don't know about you two," Ethan said. "But I rather enjoy the means."

"Amen to that," I said. "In fact..." But I hesitated. Ethan and I looked at each other. Then Kieran and I. A look, an unmistakable "I'm thinking it, but I'm not going to be the one to say it", passed between the three of us.

Ethan cleared his throat. "Well, if we all enjoy the means..." He lifted his eyebrows.

Kieran pursed his lips for a second. "I certainly have no qualms about doing it again."

"Neither do I." Ethan's eyes shifted toward me. "You?"

I ran the tip of my tongue along the inside of my lip. "More sex like that with the two of you at the same time? Count me in."

Kieran smirked as he sat up. "Well, what are we waiting for?"

"Why am I not surprised that you're ready to go again?" Ethan wiped sweat from his brow. "I don't know about either of you, but I could use a shower."

Kieran grinned. "Room for three?"

Ethan blinked. "Are you—"

"Don't tell me you've never fucked him in the shower," I said.

Ethan shook his head.

"Good God, Ethan." I ran my thumb along the side of his hand. "You're missing out."

Ethan's eyes flicked back and forth between us, then he laughed and shook his head. "You guys get the condoms, I'll get the towels."

Chapter Thirty-seven

Three Weeks Later

After Ethan set the last box in the trunk, Kieran slammed the lid and turned to us with a smile. "That's the last of it. Thanks for your help, guys."

"No problem," I said. For a moment, we passed uncertain glances around, but didn't speak.

Finally, Ethan cleared his throat. "Well, we're sorry to see you go."

Kieran smiled again. "I'm not going far. The new place is just up the street. And you still have my number."

"We fully intend to use it." I winked.

He grinned. "I look forward to it."

"And you can't go far, anyway," Ethan said. "At least not until I get my *Walk the Line* DVD back."

"Right." Kieran laughed. "I will definitely get that back to you."

"Assuming you ever watch it," I said.

"I will, I swear." Kieran grinned. "You guys will be at my housewarming, right?"

Ethan snorted. "Now there's a stupid question."

"No kidding," I said. "Consider your house duly warmed

once we get there."

Kieran thought for a moment. "You know, maybe I'll have to have a separate housewarming. You know, privately. With just you two."

"Hey, now there's an idea," Ethan said.

After a little more small talk, I said, "Well, it's getting late. I guess we should let you go."

Kieran nodded. "Yeah. Better get all of this into the house before it gets dark." He gestured at the boxes stacked in the backseat of his car.

"Call us any time," Ethan said. "You know where to find us."

"I will," Kieran said. "And if you guys come by Wilde's one night, drinks are on me."

Ethan's eyes lit up. "Body shots?"

Kieran and I both rolled our eyes, and he said, "Yeah, that's it. You know what I mean." He smiled, then kissed Ethan, drawing it out for a long moment. When they separated, he turned to me and did the same. As he pulled away, a hint of red under his collar caught my attention.

"Okay, who left that mark?" I asked. "Ethan, did you maim him again?"

Kieran reached over his shoulder. "What mark?"

"That one." I ran my finger over it. It was a faint welt, maybe an inch in length. Visible, but obviously not serious.

Ethan tugged at Kieran's collar, then laughed. "I think that was me." He tried—and failed miserably—to look sheepish. "My bad."

Kieran shrugged. "I think last night was worth a few battle scars."

"Can't argue with that," I said. "In fact, we should do it

213

again."

"We definitely will," Kieran said. Once again, he kissed us each in turn, then got in the car.

Ethan watched Kieran pull out of the driveway. "So I guess it's just us."

"So it is," I said. "Though I imagine Sabrina will be around a bit more now that classes are over."

He smiled, waving one more time to Kieran before his car disappeared around the corner. "Good. I miss having her around."

"That's not what you said when she was kicking your ass at Scrabble the other night," I laughed.

"Only because you two were cheating." He gave an exasperated sigh. "*Again.*" We both laughed, and he slid his arm around my waist. Together, we headed up the front steps.

As Ethan opened the door, I said, "You know what this means, right?"

"What's that?" He gestured for me to go ahead.

I grinned as I walked past him. "Nothing but peace and quiet in this house."

"What a pity." He grabbed my hips and pulled me back against him. His breath warmed the base of my neck as he whispered, "I think we should do something about that, don't you?"

He kicked the door shut behind us.

About the Author

To learn more about L.A. Witt, please visit www.loriawitt.com. Send an email to thethinker42@gmail.com.

GREAT
CHEAP
FUN

Discover eBooks!

THE FASTEST WAY TO GET THE HOTTEST NAMES

Get your favorite authors on your favorite reader, long before they're out in print! Ebooks from Samhain go wherever you go, and work with whatever you carry—Palm, PDF, Mobi, Kindle, nook, and more.

WWW.SAMHAINPUBLISHING.COM

CPSIA information can be obtained at www.ICGtesting.com
Printed in the USA
BVOW02s1244310116

434918BV00001BA/56/P